SERIAL KILLER Z

ALSO BY PHILIP HARRIS

Serial Killer Z

Infection (Prequel)

Serial Killer Z

Sanctuary

Shadows

Dead Isle

The Leah King Trilogy

The Leah King Trilogy Box Set

The Girl in the City

The Girl in the Wilderness

The Girl in the Machine

Glitch Mitchell

Glitch Mitchell and the Unseen Planet

Glitch Mitchell and the Island of Terror

Glitch Mitchell and the Lost Galaxy

SERIAL KILLER Z

PHILIP HARRIS

Serial Killer Z

by Philip Harris

Copyright © 2017 by Philip Harris
All rights reserved.

No part of this publication may be reproduced, stored or transmitted in any form or by any means, electronic, mechanical, recording, or otherwise, without the prior written permission of the author or publisher.

This is a work of fiction. Names, characters, places, and incidents are the product of the author's imagination. Any resemblance to actual persons, living, dead, or undead, business establishments, events, or locales is entirely coincidental.

ISBN (Print) 978-1-988968-02-5

ISBN (Ebook) 978-1-988968-03-2

12 10 9 8 7 6 5 4 3 2

Cover design by Bookfly Design

Edited by Jason Whited

Proofreading by Red Adept Editing

Even more proofreading by Pikko's House

For Ben and Duane

CONTENTS

SERIAL KILLER Z

PART I

Chapter 1
DEAD EYES

The dead man lunged across the road toward me, too-white teeth clacking as they chewed at imaginary flesh. Its eyes were sharklike black orbs, and they tracked me as I moved. Its right foot had been crushed and was dragging behind the zombie, slowing it down. Rancid breath laced with the smell of carrion and blood washed over my face and caught in my throat.

Backing away, I swung my knife at the creature's face. The blade swept across its forehead and sliced through the gray flesh. Thick black blood ran from the wound and spattered the ground at my feet. With its eyes locked on mine, the zombie took another lumbering step. My knife's handle was slick with sweat. It felt like I was trying to hold on to a fish. One wrong move, and it might break free, leaving me defenseless.

The zombie shuffled forward, clawed fingers grasping at my face. The air was thick with the smell of decay. I attacked with the knife again, an upward sweep that caught the creature's left hand and carved a deep slash in its palm. More blood sprayed across the road.

I looked past the zombie's shoulder toward the truck it had come from. My backpack was lying where I'd dropped it, beside the driver's door. It was almost empty. What little food I had was close to running out, but that bag held something far more precious. The one thing I couldn't leave behind.

A shape moved inside the truck, and another zombie reared its rotting head. It pressed its face against the glass. I groaned. Behind me, something echoed the sound.

I spun around, just in time to see another zombie reach for me—a woman dressed in jeans and an orange-and-yellow safety vest. I twisted sideways, but the creature's hands caught my shoulder. Its fingers clamped down, sinking into my flesh. A burst of pain shot down my arm. The knife slipped free and fell to the ground. Bright lights flashed across my vision.

Twisting, I wrenched my shoulder out of the female zombie's grip. The movement triggered another wave of pain. I kicked and caught its knee. There was a meaty crack as bone shattered. The joint bent sideways, and the zombie crumpled to the ground. I kicked again, this time aiming for its head. My boot caught it square on, eliciting another satisfying crack. The zombie went limp.

The first zombie reached for me. I dodged backward and retreated over the fallen woman. The zombie let out a low moan and took a couple of steps toward me. One of its feet landed on the woman's hand, and for one glorious moment, I thought it was going to fall. But it regained its balance.

My knife was lying on the ground a few feet away, half covered by the grass at the roadside. Not taking my eyes off the advancing zombie, I moved toward the knife. The creature let out a strangled moan. A thin trickle of gray fluid oozed from the side of its mouth.

My foot tapped against the knife. The zombie lunged again. I crouched and grabbed at the weapon. My hand found grass.

The zombie fell on me and knocked me over. I brought my arm up, wedging it across the creature's throat as it bore down on me. Turning my head to one side, I pushed up. The creature groaned again, and something wet and viscous spattered against my cheek. Rotten air washed over me, hot and vile. Teeth snapped at my face. I pushed again, forcing the zombie up and away as I searched blindly for the knife. My fingers brushed against something cold and hard. I grabbed it, praying it was the knife.

I swung, aiming for the side of the creature's head. Bone cracked as the knife blade sank into the zombie's neck, just below its ear. Black blood poured over my hand as I drove the knife deeper, twisting as I went. The zombie made a wet, gargling sound. I rolled sideways, sliding free, then rammed the knife harder into the thing's skull. It twitched and shook, legs bouncing against the asphalt. I pulled out the knife and scrambled away. The creature let out one last grunt, short and sharp, and was still.

I pushed myself to my feet and stood over the fallen zombies. I was shaking. It wasn't that I hadn't killed before. For their transgressions, the guilty had paid the price at my hand many times, but it was always under my terms. *I* was the one who chose the time and the place. It was a very different thing to be on a deserted highway, fighting for your life against the living dead.

And yet...

The shadow that lives inside of me came forward. It flowed through me like smoke, suffusing my body and wiping away my everyday self. That shadow has been a part of me for as long as I can remember. It gives me a unique perspective on the world and allows me to see people for what they truly are. But succumbing to the shadow leaves me exposed, vulnerable. It takes over completely, drowning my senses and opening me up to whatever dangers lurk nearby. Before the outbreak, that meant the police. Now the living dead are the biggest threat.

The shadow tightened its grip on me. The world retreated until it was as though the zombies and I were the only things in existence. My senses sharpened. The dark blood seeping into the ground became a lightless cavern. The lines on the man's face became fissures so deep I could almost feel myself falling into them. A smudge of dirt on the woman's cheek was an island floating in a sea of gray.

And then the shadow pulled back.

I could feel its disappointment as it burrowed deep inside me. The kills were necessary, but they'd also been quick and clumsy. The shadow expected more. It *needed* more. I took four deep breaths. The shadow would have to wait.

I rubbed my gore-soaked hands across the grass and willed them to stop shaking. Eventually, they did, and I returned my attention to the truck. It lay at an awkward angle with the left side tilted down to the ground. The front left tire had been removed and was now lying in a nearby ditch. The remains of a jack were scattered across the road. A dark streak swept along the truck's body as though some demented painter had splashed a can of rust-brown paint across it. Its front left corner was crumpled. A scrap of blue cloth hung from the corner of the fender.

I checked the trees behind me for signs of life then cautiously crossed the road. This part of the highway cut through the dense forest that covers large portions of the Pacific Northwest. Even before the so-called LDN-4 pandemic, you could walk for miles without seeing any signs of human civilization. That was why I'd come here in the first place—to get away from people. But there were still enough of the dead wandering around for them to be a real threat.

I'd seen how dangerous even a single zombie could be, but after six weeks of traveling, I'd grown careless. The zombie had come at me while I was checking the truck for food. It had appeared from behind the vehicle and caught me off guard. I'd almost paid the price, but I wasn't going to make the same mistake again.

As I approached the truck's cab, I heard the familiar moans of the living dead coming from inside. I grabbed my backpack. My eyes fixed on the truck's window, I pushed my hand into the bag and checked its contents. My fingers found the corner of a box. I ran them around its edge, making sure it was the leather case I was expecting, not some other container I'd forgotten about. Reassured, I moved closer to the truck.

A hand, gray and withered, slammed against the window, forcing me back a step. A moment later, the zombified remains of the truck's driver appeared. Like its hands, its face was gray. The skin was drawn tight over its skull. The trucker's hair was black, and it was a stark contrast to the pale skin. Its lips were dry and cracked. They pulled back to reveal two rows of blackened, splintered teeth. It watched me.

I leaned forward until my face was a couple of inches from the window and stared at the creature inside. I couldn't quite pull myself away. The familiar shadow stirred again. I pushed it down, stifling it for the time being. A voice, quiet but insistent, urged me to rethink what I was doing and let the shadow free. I clenched my hands into fists, digging my nails into my palms. This wasn't the place.

The truck driver let out a dull moan and then threw itself forward. Its face smashed into the window. I started and raised the knife, ready to plunge it into the creature's skull if it managed to break through.

It slammed itself against the glass again, and again. A split opened up in its forehead. Black blood smeared across the window. The corpse hit the glass again, and it cracked. The sound was unexpectedly loud in the otherwise silent forest. The creature strained against its seat belt as it tried to tear itself free. It head-butted the window again. The crack turned into a spiderweb of fractured glass.

Retreating from the truck, I reached into the backpack, checking for the box. Once I was satisfied it hadn't fallen out, I pulled the pack's drawstring closed and sealed it inside.

The driver threw itself at the truck window again, and it finally broke. Shards of glass scattered across the ground. It leaned through the opening. The seat belt across its shoulder was the only thing stopping it from crawling out to tear me apart. It moaned—a long, drawn-out cry of frustration.

I swung the backpack over my shoulder. The highway stretched out before me, winding up the mountain. The paved road was convenient, but it was also open and exposed. A few hundred feet away, a hiking trail split the forest in two. I checked back down the road. A cluster of zombies had stumbled into view in the distance. They might be a solitary group, but they could also be the vanguard of one of the swarms that tended to form along main travel routes.

They were too far away to be a real threat. Still, I'd been

following the road for too long, pushing my luck. Travel would be slower through the trees, but it would also be safer. I adjusted the position of my backpack, took four deep breaths, and walked toward the trail, the shadow within me restless and alert.

Half a mile along the hiking trail, I spotted the telltale glitter of sun reflecting off water. One of the few good things about living in the Northwest is the easy availability of water, but the weather had been hot and dry for almost a month. I checked my water bottle. It was almost empty again.

I turned south off the trail. Within a few minutes, I could hear the rush of water over rock. The ground dropped away toward a river. After six weeks in the forest, I was tired, dehydrated, and hungry. I had to stop myself from running down to the riverbank and diving into the water. There was a good chance that kind of recklessness would end up with me lying at the bottom of the slope with a broken ankle.

Still, my heartbeat quickened as I picked my way down the rocky slope to the river. I could have a bath, swim. If I was lucky, there'd be fish I could catch and eat.

When I reached the edge of the trees, I forced myself to wait. The riverbank was broad and flat. Rocks of all shapes and sizes littered the ground, everything from huge round boulders and dull gray slabs to fist-size chunks. The rocks provided plenty of places for people, living or dead, to hide. The river raced by, maddeningly close. It looked cool and refreshing. The sound of it rushing over the rocks taunted me.

I moved along the tree line, searching for signs of life and a more open area where I could see anyone trying to get near me. A few minutes up the river I found what I was looking for—an inlet fed by a much smaller river that wound through the trees and up the mountain. A flat expanse of gray rock ran around the inlet. Water lapped gently up its slope. There were fewer rocks, too. A couple were big enough to hide behind, but they were near the water. The rest were smaller than my head and certainly not large enough to provide cover. With one final check around me, I ventured out into the open.

The sun was high in the sky. I could feel it beating down on me as soon as I stepped out of the shade of the forest. I made my way to the edge of the river, crouched, and dipped my hand into the cool, clear water. I splashed some over my face then took a hesitant sip. It was cool and crisp, delicious.

I plunged my head into the river. My body clenched at the cold, and when I pulled myself out again, I was gasping for breath. I shook my head, savoring the chill, then scooped up a few more handfuls. I'd forgotten how wonderful fresh, clean water was.

I slipped off my boots and socks and sat on the edge of the rock. My feet dangled into the ice-cold water below. Within a few minutes they were numb, but I didn't care—I had clean feet.

I was considering taking my jacket and shirt off and diving in for a full-on swim when I saw a black bear and her cub. She'd wandered out of the forest on the other side of the river and was watching me closely as her cub clambered about on the rocks, occasionally drinking some water or splashing a paw at something passing by in the river. They both looked healthy enough, not that I'd seen any evidence that the contagion was capable of spreading beyond human beings.

The river was a good thirty feet wide and fast flowing. There was no chance the bear was going to be able to get to me quickly, but I kept a wary eye on her, just in case. The cub stumbled across the rocks and bumped into its mother's leg. She looked down at him, letting out a little snort. The cub bounced away, distracted by something down at the river's edge.

The bear turned toward the forest and lifted her head, sniffing at the air. A few seconds later, I heard the helicopter myself.

Chapter 2
FLYBY

Cursing, I pulled my feet out of the water, grabbed my boots and socks, and half ran, half hopped across the rock to the trees. I ducked out of sight just as a chopper swept over the forest. It was military, the sort of aircraft I'd seen in a dozen Vietnam War films. It even had a soldier sitting in the open doorway, manning a belt-fed machine gun. Presumably, that was for dealing with swarms of zombies.

The swarms were one reason I preferred to keep to the forest, off the beaten path. The other was to avoid the military and other groups of survivors. Hard though my life might be, I had no interest in being rescued.

The chopper came in low and banked to the right, spraying water across the rocks and shaking the trees. I covered my face to protect myself from the dust and debris being blown around. Someone had painted a cartoon caricature of a zombie head on the aircraft's nose. It had an ax embedded in its skull and the words "Aim for the Brain" written around it.

It looked as though the pilot was going to land on a flat

outcrop of rock. I nervously looked for a better place to hide. Then the engine noise increased in pitch, and the chopper roared off up the river. A few seconds later, it disappeared out of sight around a bend. I waited until the sound of its engine had faded away completely before coming out of my hiding place.

The bear and her cub had gone.

I went back to the edge of the rocks and looked at the water. It was so cool and inviting. I hadn't had a shower since leaving the city, and I stank almost as bad as the living dead.

Not wanting to be caught in the open if the helicopter came back, I settled for taking off my jacket and shirt. I rinsed the dirt and gore from them as best I could and splashed water over my arms and chest. Then, reluctantly, I turned my back to the river and watched the forest for signs of life while the sun dried my clothes.

A dragonfly droned past my ear, snapping me awake. I was tired, and the sun's heat was making me lethargic. That was dangerous. I dunked my head into the water to clear it then pulled on my shirt and jacket.

A light breeze drifted across the inlet, and I let the clean air and the sound of the water wash over me. It all seemed so idyllic. I could almost convince myself I wasn't living through a global catastrophe that might prove to be the human race's extinction event. But I was, and I kept an eye on the horizon and the forest around me, even as I enjoyed the scenery.

I'd been sitting there for ten or fifteen minutes when I caught a movement out of the corner of my eye. Someone was walking through the forest, picking their way between the trees toward the water. And they were on my side of the river.

Chapter 3

TEMPTATION CALLS

Whoever it was, they hadn't seen me yet. I ducked down behind the boulder, low enough that I was almost out of sight but still had a view of the bank.

A few seconds later, a young man broke out of the trees and ran to the river's edge. He threw himself down on the rocks, hard enough to make me flinch, and began scooping water into his mouth. His clothes, blue jeans and a T-shirt that had probably once been white, were ripped and covered in dirt. His hair was matted and clung to his head, and his face was cut. Blood from the wound had run down his cheek and neck, staining the T-shirt. He had no equipment. No backpack, canteen, or weapons.

The man lapped hungrily at the water. He was trying to drink too quickly, and his body couldn't keep up. He started coughing and spluttering so hard I thought he might vomit. But he didn't, and as soon as he got himself under control again, he plunged his hands back into the river and continued drinking.

As I watched him, a familiar coldness grew inside me—the stirring of the shadow. And with the shadow came insight. The man's guilt hung off him as tattered strips of oily blackness. He wiped his face and left black smears across his cheek. He plunged his hands into the water again, and a black film spread across the surface. My throat turned dry, and it became hard to swallow. Sweat coated my hands.

Eventually, the young man stopped drinking. He lay back on the rocks, one arm resting across his forehead. I could see his chest rising and falling, his breathing quick and heavy. The shadow sent a shudder rippling through me.

The man was a hundred feet or so away and close to the tree line. It would be a simple matter to circle unseen through the forest until I was directly behind him. I could be on him before he knew I was there. It would be so easy. There was no one to stop me.

The shadow rose up. Ice-cold tendrils weaved through my body like a dozen snakes. I felt something cold in my hand and looked down. It was my hunting knife, although I couldn't remember how it got there. I blinked at it. The blade called to me. I raised it in front of my face. The sun glinted off its tip as I twisted it left and right. I imagined the young man, the knife pressed against the side of his throat. I saw it cut into his flesh, releasing a thin trickle of scarlet blood.

I fought back, stifling the shadow's urges. It was a risk I couldn't take. I took a deep breath and closed my eyes. I wish I could say my actions were motivated by some moral code—kitchen table ethics that had been drilled into me by a caring father. But my father had left us when I was six or seven, for good reason as far as I could tell. My motivations for not killing were purely selfish. The shadow was already deadening my awareness of the world around me. Giving in to its urges would leave me completely exposed.

I forced myself to look away from the knife. And the

young man. The shadow writhed. I pushed it down, driving it into the darkest recesses of my body. I'd find a way to quell the shadow without putting myself at risk.

Inhaling deeply, I counted to four then put the knife back into the sheath on my belt. I grabbed the palm of my left hand with my right and squeezed. Long nails dug into the soft flesh. I focused on the pain, acknowledging it, letting it suffuse my whole body. The shadow retreated.

When I let go of my hand, there was a semicircle of indentations in my flesh. I'd pressed hard enough to break the skin in a couple of places. My palm was smeared with blood.

The young man was sitting up now. He was looking around as though he'd realized how exposed he was. A normal person, a good person, would have tried to help him. They'd wave to him, call him over, try to convince him they weren't a threat and that the two of them would be safer traveling together. And they'd be right. A lone man traveling through the forest was an easy target—for the living or the dead. By the look of him he'd been on the run for some time, and it was a miracle that he hadn't already fallen afoul of a predator of one form or another.

But I wasn't a good person. Not even close. He was better off alone, for both our sakes.

The young man took another drink from the river then stood on shaky legs. He looked around, and I thought that maybe I'd been mistaken. Perhaps he did have some equipment after all. He was squinting as he peered left and right, and I wondered if he was nearsighted. Another reason for a good person to help him. I just hoped he'd choose to go in the direction that would lead him away from me.

In the end, he did. I watched him make his way up the river. His progress was slow and unsteady on the rocky bank. He walked without paying the slightest bit of attention to the world around him. I had no idea how he'd survived this long. Maybe he'd been with someone until very recently. I watched after him even after he disappeared around a corner, trying and failing to feel some emotion.

A loud crack from across the river broke the spell. It was probably just an old branch breaking or an animal. Maybe it was the bear and her cub coming back. I took it as a sign to move on. I refilled the water bottles from my pack and considered my options.

Part of me wanted to stay with the river. Ease of movement and the abundance of food and water, not to mention the opportunity to bathe, made it a tempting option. But it was exposed. If I thought it was a good idea to travel alongside the water, so would other people. It might seem like it most of the time, but I wasn't the only refugee wandering the forest. In the end, I compromised and headed up the inlet, following the path of the smaller river as it wound steadily north.

The slope on this part of the mountain was fairly shallow, and I made good progress. As I walked, I gradually began to relax. My spirits rose. I'd beaten the shadow again, twice in one day. It had been gaining strength over the past few weeks as my nomadic lifestyle wore me down, but I'd shown myself that I could still resist. Eventually, I would need to sate its appetite, but that was a problem I could deal with later, on my own terms.

About half a mile up the river, I spotted a wooden gateway on the opposite bank. Nature had camouflaged it well, and I almost walked right past it. The trail beyond was partially overgrown, still passable but clearly unused for some time. Lush green vines obscured the gateposts. A sign was attached to the top of the posts, but it was so overgrown with ivy that it took me some time to decipher the words carved into it.

CAMP REDFERN

I glanced up and down the river. The forest was quiet. I could afford a detour.

Chapter 4

REDFERN

I followed the trail for a couple of hundred yards but left it before I reached the camp's entrance. Instead, I picked my way carefully between the trees until I could see the camp and then positioned myself behind some bushes that did a pretty good job of keeping me hidden. Then I waited.

Camp Redfern looked deserted. Four wooden single-story cabins sat in a semicircle, two on each side of a fifth two-story building. A carved sign in the same style as the archway at the river hung above the bigger building's door, declaring it to be THE LODGE. It was built on a raised wooden platform. Three steps led up to a walkway that ran along the front of the building and was home to two wooden chairs. I half expected John Wayne to come charging out, six-shooters blazing, cutting down zombies left and right as they chased him out of the lodge.

A pair of objects shrouded in dusty black tarpaulins, and what looked like a generator, sat on one side of the lodge. A large stack of firewood was piled on the other. Beyond the generator were two small sheds. One had a large M painted on the door in white, the other a W.

The main entrance to the camp was directly opposite my hiding place. A wide track led into the forest. The ground was dry and dusty but heavily rutted. Grass and weeds had begun to reclaim the track.

A fire pit sat in the middle of the clearing in front of the buildings. The earth around it was burned black. By the look of the lumps of charred wood lying in the pit, it had been used fairly recently. Four benches, each just three pieces of wood fixed together in a simple H shape, were arranged around the fire. A white plate sat on one of them, and another lay on the ground near the pit.

A soft moan floated across the camp. It took me a few seconds to find the sound's source because the zombie that had made it was lying on the ground on the opposite side of the fire pit.

Its entire lower body was missing. All that remained were a few ragged, bloody scraps hanging from its waist. It was wearing overalls, blue and oil-stained. By the look of the trail it had left behind, the zombie had dragged itself along the track to get to the camp and had stopped just short of the fire pit. It moaned again, moving its head from side to side, and I wondered if it had somehow caught my scent. If it had, it would come for me. Flesh is food as far as the living dead are concerned.

The creature let out another groan and struggled to raise its head. There was no way of knowing how long it had been in the camp. If there were people living there, they'd have surely killed the zombie if they'd seen it. Which meant either it hadn't been there long, or the camp was unoccupied.

I crouched in the forest and watched the lodge for signs of life until my legs started going numb. I shivered. The sun was going down, and pretty soon it'd be dark.

The buildings still seemed devoid of life. The camp reminded me of a documentary on ghost towns of the Americas I'd watched a few months earlier, long before the outbreak had begun creating ghost towns of its own. Even the zombie had stopped trying to move and was lying on the ground, murmuring softly to itself.

I looked at the forest around me. I usually spent my nights up a tree. It was the best way to avoid an encounter with the forest's wildlife or any wandering undead. I've always intended to die in my sleep, but I'm trying to delay it for as long as possible. A few feet behind me there was a pine that looked climbable.

My other option was to explore the lodge. If it was empty, there'd be a place to sleep. Maybe even clean sheets. A ripple of pleasure ran down my spine at the thought. I didn't dare imagine a working shower. But the camp had obviously been occupied recently. I'd spent the last few weeks avoiding my fellow survivors as carefully as I avoided the dead. I should resist the temptation of the camp, move on. That shadow part of me disagreed. If there were people living here, it would deal with them.

I spent another thirty minutes watching the lodge and battling with myself over the right course of action. Eventually, the growing darkness forced me to make a decision. I pushed my way back to the trail and walked into the camp.

As soon as it saw me, the bisected zombie grew agitated and started dragging itself toward me. It moaned and ground its teeth together as though it had already ripped a chunk of meat from my calf. One of its eyes was missing. The other tracked me as I walked across the clearing.

I removed my knife from its sheath. The zombie's moans became louder and more insistent the closer I got. It strained toward me, mouth open. A ribbon of blackish drool rolled over its bottom lip and dripped to the ground. It stank —a mix of rancid meat, blood, and its own waste. Black bile leaked from its stomach.

As I pulled the knife back, ready to plunge it into the zombie's skull, the shadow stopped me. The sight of the mindless creature struggling to get at me had piqued its interest. There was a thread of something here, a fundamental truth that I'd missed so far.

I stood transfixed as the zombie clawed at the ground, pulling itself closer, inch by inch. When it got too near, I took half a step backward. Like the carrot on the stick, I was always just out of reach. No matter how hard the zombie worked, the end result would always be failure and death. It seemed a perfect metaphor for life.

The zombie let out a frustrated moan and stretched its neck toward me. Its fingers scraped across the ground, nails tearing free. Joints cracked, and flecks of blood splashed across the earth as it snapped and snarled. It strained to get close enough to sink its teeth into me, the tendons in its neck standing taut. The zombie pulled itself forward again. Its ribs caught on a rock and cracked. Pushing the shadow's protestations away, I plunged the knife into the top of the zombie's head. It broke through and sank into its brain.

I pulled my knife free, and the zombie rolled sideways. It thrashed and writhed. Its arms flailed. Black stains splashed across the ground from its wounds. It screamed—a high-pitched wailing that had me covering my ears.

I was afraid the sound would attract more of the dead, so I slammed the knife into the side of the thing's neck and twisted. The blade cut through muscle and bone and into the corpse's throat. The screaming stopped as its vocal cords were shredded. It twitched and convulsed for a few more seconds then lay still.

I rolled the corpse over. Its one good eye stared lifelessly up into the sky, looking for all the world like a perfectly black marble. The logo over its heart labeled it as an employee of Jim's Garage. A name was embroidered on the opposite side in white cursive letters—Eric. I wiped the knife on its overalls before putting it away.

The wooden decking in front of the lodge was stained with a dark reddish-brown patch roughly the size of a human being. The stain was dry and faded in places as though it had been there long enough for rain to begin washing it away.

I circled around the stain to the lodge's entrance and stood in front of the door. It was already ajar but not enough for me to see inside. The building was silent. I counted to sixteen then tensed, ready to run if anything came lumbering out of the lodge toward me. I nudged the door with my foot. It creaked like something out of an old horror movie as it swung open, revealing a darkened room.

With one final look around the camp, I walked inside.

Chapter 5

BLOOD AND DUST

There were light switches just inside the door, but I didn't want to give away my arrival by turning them on. So, I waited until my eyes had adjusted to the gloom.

I was in an open, lounge-like space. There were blinds over the windows that filtered out the setting sun and gave everything a murky beige tint. The air smelled of cut wood, but a darker scent lay beneath it. Something coppery and rotten.

A fireplace sat at the right-hand end of the room. There was a metal cradle of neatly stacked firewood beside it, and a few scraps of burned wood lay in the bottom of the grate.

Clustered around the fire were a long couch and two armchairs. Their oak frames were rough but well built. The cushions, though faded through use, were thick and looked comfortable. Even if there wasn't a bed I could use, the couch would be a step up from a tree. A low coffee table sat between the chairs. Its modern metal-and-glass design contrasted awkwardly with the rustic styling of the rest of the furniture.

A battered leather jacket was draped over the arm of one

of the chairs. An equally well-worn paperback sat on the table. I didn't recognize the author, but by the look of the cover it was a romance. That might be a good sign. Roving gangs of post-apocalyptic bandits are rarely fans of bodice rippers. At least not in the movies.

A staircase led up to a balcony that overlooked the lounge. A set of five pictures hung on the wall beside the stairs. They were photographs, each one showing a group of three people standing in similar poses outside the lodge. To the left of the stairs there was another door. It was open, and through it I could see a long dining table flanked by chairs. There were no signs of movement.

I closed my eyes and listened, trying to pick up any signs of life. All I could hear was the occasional chatter of birds outside. Unable to stall any longer, I walked as lightly as I could toward the dining room, running my fingers over the red cloth of the couch as I passed it.

The book was indeed a romance, and the leather jacket was designed for a woman and was free of any kind of biker gang markings. Another good sign. In fact, everything seemed normal. It would have felt perfectly reasonable for a group of teenagers to walk past me into the lodge, fresh from a hike through the forest, chattering about the owls or the bears or the eagles they'd seen. There were no signs of a struggle. No dismembered corpses. But the stain on the walkway outside, and the trace of decay in the air, told a different story.

The dining room held more signs of everyday life. The long table was oak and set for four people, although there were six chairs. The plates and cutlery were covered in a fine film of dust.

A notebook sat at the end of the table, open to a blank page. It was a diary. I flicked back to the beginning. It started a couple of weeks before the outbreak. Whoever had written it was already living in the lodge when the rest of the world went to hell. I skimmed through the entries, looking for mention of the pandemic, but there weren't any. The last entry in the diary was eight days earlier. Up until that point, everything had apparently been normal. From the names mentioned in the diary, the camp had been occupied by at least half a dozen people—three counselors and three students. The adults and their charges had spent their days exploring the forest, learning new skills and bonding. There was nothing about the living dead.

Another long oak table stood against the left-hand wall. It ran below three windows, one of which was strung with an impressive-looking cobweb. A selection of bowls stood on top of the table. All of them were empty. There was an old radio next to them, its antenna extended. Without thinking, I flicked the power switch and got the hiss of static. I flinched and turned the radio off.

Someone had left a half-full coffee mug on the table. Its contents were beginning to take on a life of their own. A large frame containing a yellowing photograph of a group of eight teenagers and four adults hung on the opposite wall. The caption beneath the photograph read: Camp Redfern Opens, 1994.

A breeze wafted through an open window in the far wall, cooling the room. The smell of decay was lighter here, presumably because of the air coming in through the window. I twisted open the blinds on the other windows to give me a little more light. I had a flashlight and a healthy supply of batteries, but that didn't mean I wanted to waste them.

Beside the open window, there were two doors. One, the rear entrance to the lodge, led directly outside. The other was a two-way door with a small round window in it, like they have in restaurants.

I peered outside. There was no walkway on this side of the building, just a grassy clearing and then a wall of trees where the camp gave way to the forest. There were four sets of muddy hiking boots lined up next to a bench.

A bolt was fixed to the top of the door, but it was unlocked. I toyed with the idea of going outside, but it was getting dark and I wanted to finish exploring the lodge while I could still see.

I turned my attention to the other door and gently pushed it open.

The kitchen beyond came with the basics—an electric stove, a fridge, and an old enamel sink. A square counter sat in the middle of the room with a very new-looking coffee maker sitting on it. Otherwise, the appliances looked old enough to have been installed when the camp first opened. A large saucepan sat on the stove, but the rest of the pots and pans, seven of them, hung from hooks attached to the ceiling above the counter.

I checked the fridge. It wasn't running, but the inside was still cool, and there was food. Real food. Carrots, apples, a couple of bars of chocolate, and even a half-full carton of milk. I sniffed the milk and gagged. The fruit didn't look much better. Cupboards around the walls held a few cleaning supplies and more food—canned and dried goods and yet more energy bars.

I tried the faucets. Clear water sputtered into the sink. I cupped my hands and drank a little. The water had an earthy undertaste, but otherwise, it was good. I turned off the faucets again. I had no idea how long the clean water would last, and it was a luxury I didn't want to waste.

I went back to the lounge and stood beside the armchair

with the leather jacket. It seemed that at some point in the recent past there had been at least four people in the lodge, and they'd seemingly been completely oblivious to what was happening back in the real world. I idly picked up the jacket and pressed it against my face. The smell of clean leather and a subtle hint of flowery perfume overwhelmed the lingering smell of rot for a few seconds.

There was still a chance the camp's occupants weren't in the lodge. Maybe they'd heard about the pandemic and gone home to their families. Even as the idea occurred to me, I knew it was wrong. They were upstairs.

The hint of blood and decay I'd smelled in the lounge grew stronger as I climbed the stairs. I looked at the photographs as I passed in an effort to delay myself. They were all pictures of the "Camp Redfern Leaders" from 1994 onward. Each photo showed two men and a woman. One of the men and the woman were different in every image, but Dominic Suter was present in all of them, steadily growing older. The last photo, John Wrigley, Mary Kelson, and Dominic Suter, was dated 2012.

I'm sure it was just my overworked imagination, but the air seemed thicker the higher I climbed. By the time I got to the balcony, it felt like I was pushing through molasses. My heart rate increased with every step. My throat was dry. I considered stopping to get a drink from my backpack, but that might have been all the opportunity my subconscious needed to send me heading down the stairs and back into the forest.

There were three doors leading off the balcony. All of them were closed, and I felt like a Monty Hall contestant trying to guess which door held the cash prize and which would earn me a goat. Or in my case, a reanimated corpse. There were no signs of life from beyond the doors. If it hadn't been for the smell of death in the air, I could prob-ably have convinced myself the rooms were empty.

"Hello?" I said.

Hearing my voice was strange. I hadn't spoken anything coherent aloud for weeks. I've never been one for idle chat-ter, and parties are my personal definition of hell, but it still felt odd not talking.

When no one responded, I called again—louder this time. Still, I got no response, so I knocked on the first door. "Is anyone in there?"

Silence.

I pulled out my hunting knife and spent a few seconds checking my grip, making sure I wasn't going to drop it should a rotting corpse leap out at me. Unable to think of any more ways to procrastinate, I swung the door open and looked inside.

The room was small and held just a single bed, a wardrobe, and a tiny dressing table with a chair in front of it. It was also a complete mess. Clothes were strewn across the floor. The bed was unmade—sheets tangled together and abandoned. One of the pillows was lying diagonally across the bed; the other was wedged into one corner of the room as though someone had thrown it there. A black bra was draped across the chair.

A pink suitcase lay open beneath the room's solitary window. Its contents, mostly pastel T-shirts, underwear, and a pair of black jeans, looked like they were trying to escape. The tip of a white shirt poked out from between the wardrobe doors.

It was hard to tell whether the room had been ransacked by an intruder or simply belonged to someone who cared more about having fun than keeping their room tidy. Either way, there were no corpses, reanimated or otherwise.

I took a couple of steps into the room, and although I don't really know why, I called out again. Just a quiet "Hello."

Maybe I thought some prankster was going to come bounding out of the wardrobe at me. When that didn't happen, I went back out to the balcony and moved on to the second room. I paused, holding the door handle and listening for signs of movement from inside for a few seconds. Then I swung the door open.

The smell of blood was stronger here, and a handful of flies buzzed fitfully about the room, but there were no bodies. Size and layout wise, the room was an identical copy of the first. Same single bed, same wardrobe, dressing table, and chair. But that was where the similarities ended. Whereas the first room had shown every sign of being the site of a remarkably localized tornado, this one was evidently home to the world's most anal-retentive human being.

The bed was neatly made, pillows fluffed, sheets drawn tight and tucked in—hospital corners, of course. Two books were stacked neatly on the dressing table, both hardback. One was by Junot Diaz, the other David Mitchell. There were two suitcases, black and sleek-looking, standing in one corner. Accident or not, they were perfectly aligned with each other. Even the padlocks hung at the same angle. There were no shirts peering from between the wardrobe doors, no discarded underwear. In fact, there was barely any sign of occupancy at all. Take away the suitcases and the books, and you'd think the room was waiting for its guest to arrive.

This time, I didn't bother calling out.

I'll take door number three, Monty.

The smell hit me as soon as I opened the door. The

stench of decay was so strong I had to cover my mouth and force myself not to throw up. A cluster of flies swarmed at me. They bounced across my face, and one almost flew into my eye before I waved them away.

Later, it would register that the third room was bigger, with a matching double bed and cabinets as well as the dressing table and wardrobe. But all I saw that first visit were the bodies.

There were three of them. Two, a man and a woman, were lying on the bed. Their fingers were intertwined. I recognized them from the photographs on the stairs—John Wrigley and Mary Kelson. The third body, Dominic Suter, was in a chair in front of the window, facing out toward the forest.

At first, I thought the two on the bed were uninjured. They looked almost serene, as though they might just be asleep. Empty sleeping-pill bottles on the cabinet nearby added to the illusion, but they each had a hole in their foreheads.

The wounds were perfectly round. Tracks of dried blood ran down the side of their heads and pooled on the pillows around them. A bloodied screwdriver sat on the cabinet next to the bottles, and there was a discarded hammer on the floor. Based on the lack of decay, they hadn't been dead long, but dozens of flies buzzed around the room and crawled over the bodies.

Dominic Suter hadn't died as neatly. He was holding a hunting rifle, the barrel still caught on his bottom jaw. A chunk was missing from the back of his head. Bits of skull and brain were clearly visible through the ragged opening. Gore spattered the rug on the floor behind him, and the chair was streaked with dried blood. More flies crawled over

Suter's wound, and a few white maggots writhed and twisted in the cavity the bullet had left behind.

I stared at the bodies. I should have felt some emotion for them, but I didn't. Yes, the blood and the smell and the flies repulsed me, but that was all. I felt no pity, no sadness at the senseless loss of life. Not even anger that they'd chosen the easy way out. I didn't care that they'd taken their own lives instead of fighting to survive.

It wasn't until the fact that there were only three bodies really sank in that I felt anything.

I tensed, the familiar ache of low-grade fear that accompanied life in a zombie-infested world intensified. I walked slowly into the room, picking my way around the gore until I could see past the bed properly. I think I was hoping to find a fourth body lying on the floor, but there was nothing there. I crouched down, trying to look beneath the bed, but the covers hung too low. A dozen horror movie scenes flashing through my head, I reached out and lifted up the covers. Nothing.

Despite how ridiculous the idea of a zombie hiding inside a piece of furniture seemed, I still felt a cold trickle of fear running down my spine as I swung open the wardrobe door. A handful of shirts hung on wooden hangers. I pushed them aside, checking the corners of the wardrobe, then closed it.

The fear eased, replaced by the weight of an unfinished puzzle. The sights and smells of the death around me faded into the background as I thought about my exploration of the lodge, searching for the hiding place I'd missed. There were a dozen places I hadn't checked.

Flies buzzed around my face, snapping me out of my reverie. Outside, the light was fading. The room felt darker, its shadows deeper. I swatted at the flies as I turned away from the corpses and left the room.

Maybe I hadn't checked the other two rooms properly. I rummaged around inside my backpack until I found my flashlight. Knife in one hand, the flashlight in the other, I went back into the middle room and searched it. Thoroughly this time.

When I was finally satisfied nothing lurked under the bed or in the wardrobe, I did the same with the first room. I had to move clothes and bedsheets aside and drag a pile of dirty washing from beneath the bed before I could be sure it, too, was empty, but eventually I felt comfortable it was clear.

I went back onto the balcony and looked down at the lounge. The vantage point gave me a better view of the room, and I swept the flashlight around, chasing away the shadows. The light played over the door, illuminating the dark stain on the walkway.

I let out an anguished groan. I'd left the door open. The lodge had been easily accessible, exposed, all the time I'd been checking the rooms. My brain ran through a dozen scenarios as I charged down the stairs. None of them were good.

I kicked the door closed, hard enough to rattle the frame. The door had a lock, but there was no sign of the key. I had to make do with the single bolt at the top of the door. Painfully aware of the fading light, I moved through the lounge, checking for signs of an intruder.

A noise came from the direction of the kitchen—the sound of metal clattering against metal. I adjusted the grip on my knife and moved cautiously into the dining room.

The bigger windows and open blinds provided a little more light, and I was fairly sure the room was empty. After a cursory check beneath the table, I moved toward the kitchen. As I passed the back door, I looked outside. The patch of grass certainly looked empty, but the forest beyond could have held an army of the living dead in its shadows. I slid the bolt on the back door.

In contrast to the dining room, the kitchen was almost completely dark. The pots and pans hanging from the ceiling cast eerie shadows across the walls as I swept my flashlight around the room. Most of the kitchen was visible from the doorway, and my panic eased slightly as it became clear that it was empty, too. I checked under the kitchen table and then took a few paces into the room, moving around the edge so that I could see beyond the fridge.

I saw the flash of a figure pressed up against the wall. And then the light burned the shadows away, and all that remained was an empty vegetable rack and a broom. I checked the pans hanging from the ceiling again. All seven were there, and the eighth was still sitting on top of the stove.

I made my way around the kitchen again, slower this time, looking under the table, opening the cupboards one by one. Finally satisfied the kitchen was secure, I moved back out to the dining room and did the same. I made sure the back door and the windows were locked, shone the light beneath the table, and searched the shadows until I was convinced that room was empty, too.

The lounge was next. Again, I checked the corners and beneath the table and chairs. I paused for a moment by the leather jacket. It had been moved. When I'd arrived, it was draped over the arm of one of the chairs. Now it was lying on the table. I picked it up and remembered. I'd put it there myself. Sighing, I put the jacket where it had been when I'd first arrived. The fireplace was narrow, probably too small for someone to hide in. I shone the light up into the blackness of the chimney anyway.

Then I stood in the middle of the lounge, mentally ticking off each room in turn and locking away my fear that someone had slipped into the lodge while I was upstairs. I glanced toward the balcony. The doors were still closed, but I had to stop myself from checking the rooms again. I was taking things too far. Letting my paranoia run rampant. The world might be out to get me, but the lodge was empty. Safe.

I sat down and looked through my backpack, searching for my case. It was still there. The soft leather beneath my fingertips eased my paranoia. I let out a deep breath and closed the backpack. I flicked off the flashlight and let the gloom swallow me up. There were still four cabins to explore, each one a potential home to the living or the dead, but that could wait until morning.

A faint bubble of excitement formed in my stomach. After so long trailing through the forest with no real goal and no guarantee that I'd find a safe place to sleep, let alone food or water, I'd found a sanctuary. Maybe it was even a place I could call home. The camp was small enough that I could set up a perimeter to warn me if anything wandered in from the forest. Something simple, like tin cans on a string. It wouldn't help me against more intelligent threats, humans with a pulse, but the idea of having a bed to sleep in, running water, and a supply of food was too good to ignore.

I'd have to deal with the bodies upstairs, and soon. Even if I moved into one of the cabins, it would be foolish to leave three rotting corpses lying around. And that was assuming impaling the dead's brain with a screwdriver was enough to prevent them from coming back to life.

And there was the matter of the fourth inhabitant of the

lodge. Unless I'd miscounted, there were four sets of boots by the back door. Somewhere there was another body... or a zombie. And the diary had hinted at two other people. I tried to put the thought out of my mind. I was as sure as I could be that I was alone inside the lodge, but the idea of another zombie wandering around somewhere made me uncomfortable. They'd probably left to go and get help or wandered off into the forest, searching for prey. Maybe the man I'd seen by the river was the missing camper. Either way, I'd have to get used to the uncertainty.

I decided to spend the night on the couch. It was comfortable, and the idea of sleeping near the corpses upstairs made me uneasy. I'm not squeamish—how could I be with the shadow's ever-present influence shaping my life? It was simply prudent to keep a safe distance away from potential threats. I put a couple of the chairs from the dining room on the staircase as an early warning system and then lay down.

Even with all my precautions, I struggled to get to sleep. My mind replayed the day's events—the zombies on the road, the man by the river, the bodies. Again and again, the images flashed through my head like a holiday slideshow. The lodge creaked and rattled as it settled around me, and I wondered if I really had checked the rooms properly. Had I missed a corner or a cupboard, or maybe a closet?

I opened the top of my backpack and made sure the leather case was still there. Even then, I couldn't settle, only managing to snatch five or ten minutes here and there when my tumbling thoughts eased up enough to let me doze. The sky outside was already beginning to lighten before I finally calmed myself enough to fall into a real, deep sleep.

Chapter 6

CABINS IN THE WOODS

Waking up in the lodge left me disoriented and uncertain. The shreds of a nightmare filled with a horde of ravenous corpses clung to me like morning cobwebs. The room I was in seemed utterly unfamiliar. For a few seconds, I was convinced I might actually have dreamed the pandemic. Then reality seeped into my consciousness, and it all came flooding back. Along with the realization I needed to pee.

The two sheds I'd noticed when I first arrived in the camp were outhouses. Like the rest of the buildings, they were well made, solid. Whoever had built this place had taken pride in their work. Like they'd wanted the camp to last.

The women's outhouse had bright flowers painted on the inside of the door, the men's a selection of clichéd, and clean, graffiti with a couple of groan-worthy knock-knock jokes thrown in for good measure. I wondered whether the shed's creator would approve of the decorations that had been added to their legacy.

The toilets were really just a plastic seat over a hole in

the ground, probably leading to a septic tank. Hand-painted signs reminded occupants not to put non-biodegradable materials into the toilet. In particular, condoms were cited as especially problematic. Next to each toilet, separated by a varnished wooden screen, was a shower. They both worked, although the water was cold.

A standpipe stood outside each shed, a misshapen soap on a rope hanging from the women's. I spent a good half hour in the men's latrine—a simple thing like toilet paper becomes a treat of epic proportions when civilization falls apart. A shower, even a freezing-cold one, is an incomparable luxury. When I finally stepped out, I felt clean and refreshed. Putting on my old clothes took away some of the pleasure, and I made a note to check the bedrooms for anything that would fit me.

Back in the lodge, I had a breakfast of peanut butter and apple. It was a welcome change from jerky, Chinese Bar-B-Q flavor or otherwise.

I ate quickly while the shadow berated me for wasting so much time. I still needed to check the rest of the camp. There were four more cabins that held who knew what—zombies, maybe the missing campers. Or maybe there'd be more food or equipment I could use. And if the camp was clear and I really was going to stay here, I'd need to get the bodies out of the room upstairs.

As soon as I finished the food, I went out to the cabins. From the outside, all four were identical. Wooden numbers nailed above the doors were the only distinguishing feature. Inside was a completely different story. The furniture was standard—two bunk beds, a couch, an armchair, a chest of drawers big enough to hide a body in, and a coffee table. All of it matched the wooden furniture in the lodge. But beyond that, each cabin had been decorated in a radically different style.

Cabin one was painted with subtle pastel colors, blues and greens mostly. The beds were draped with soft, green covers, and the gray seating had been livened up with a handful of scattered cushions in more pastel shades. A wooden frame was attached to one wall, and the painting inside it showed a landscape of rolling green hills beneath a gloriously blue sky. It created the illusion that the viewer was looking out through a window. The painting itself was unexpectedly good, and the effect was remarkable, soothing almost.

There were no signs of any occupants. Everything was in its place, and there were no cases or clothes lying around. The chest of drawers was empty.

The second cabin was almost the complete opposite of the first. It looked more like a garage than a place someone would want to sleep. The walls were covered with discarded bicycle parts. Everything from wheels to chains, handlebars, and even a full bike frame. Four old snowboards, scratched and dented, hung from the ceiling. A stack of battered skateboarding, bicycle, and skiing helmets stood in one corner. The pile reached almost to the ceiling and leaned at a precarious angle. Everything in the room was damaged—scratched, bent, or broken in some way. The chest of drawers, bed, couch, and even the floor had been artfully gouged and scraped.

As if that wasn't enough, the walls had been covered with graffiti in a sense-assaulting kaleidoscope of colors. I couldn't read most of it, although the wall that had been painted as a window in cabin one had KA-BOOM BOX painted on it in letters that were taller than me.

The bedcovers were made from dozens of T-shirts

stitched together. I recognized some of the bands on the shirts from my teenage years, and others were classic rock bands that spanned multiple generations. The rest I'd never heard of.

The cabin was as unoccupied as the first, and judging from the dust on every surface, I'd been the first person inside it for quite some time.

Cabin three did have signs of being used. It didn't really have a theme, just a bright color scheme with a few abstract prints and a multicolored blanket thrown over the couch for good measure. There were three suitcases, two matching hard shells and a third, much larger gray case that looked as though it had been through one too many baggage-handling systems. The cat-shaped luggage tags on the hard cases read Ruby Donaldson, while the battered one had belonged to Clara-Jane Welch.

The cases themselves were empty. The contents had been neatly folded and placed in the chest of drawers. I guessed the top two drawers belonged to Ruby—their contents included a long nightshirt with Purrrrfect and a picture of a smug-looking cat on it. Her clothes were practical but smart. Clara-Jane, on the other hand, had favored a more eclectic wardrobe of well-worn T-shirts, faded denim jeans and shorts, a couple of thin blouses, and a white skirt.

The rest of the cabin had a lived-in feel. Bedcovers weren't quite straight, couch cushions were squashed, that sort of thing. But the layer of dust was still there. Ruby and Clara-Jane hadn't been in the cabin for several weeks.

The fourth and final cabin had been decorated using every hippie cliché you can imagine. Psychedelic swirls covered the walls along with sprawling, bubbly graffiti phrases like Peace Out and Love Is, Man. Variations of the ubiquitous yellow smiley were plastered everywhere, including a single giant one with multicolored spirals for eyes that dominated the ceiling and made me dizzy just looking at it.

The bunk beds had patchwork quilts draped over them that broke every rule of good interior design. Each square of the quilts was a different color. Hearts, swirls and yet more smiley faces had been sewn onto most of them. The result was so disorientating I had difficulty believing anyone would be able to sleep with one of the quilts in sight.

But someone had, because this cabin had also been occupied. There were four suitcases this time, three black cloth ones that looked brand new and a large brown one that didn't. An old wooden trunk sat at the foot of one of the beds. Its lid was curved, and that, combined with the metal bands that held it together, made it look a lot like a pirate's treasure chest. It wasn't locked. When I opened it, I found half a dozen old horror paperbacks, a few blankets, and some leather notebooks similar to the one I'd found in the lodge, but empty. There was no fortune in gold doubloons.

The brown case didn't have a label, but the black ones did. They belonged to one Arlo Chan, from Vancouver, and were empty apart from a couple of spare address labels.

Whoever owned the brown case hadn't bothered to unpack. The contents were a jumbled mess of T-shirts, jeans, socks, and men's underwear. A faint smoky smell hung in the air near the case—cigarettes rather than cigars. When I leaned closer, I got a whiff of the same smell.

The stale air was starting to give me a headache, but I checked the chest of drawers. Inside, there were six neat stacks of clothes. I pulled out a pair of jeans. They were fairly new and looked roughly my size. There were shirts, too. I found a plain blue one that looked like it might fit along with some underwear and a black T-shirt. I almost changed then and there, but I still needed to move the bodies.

Fresh clothes in hand, I went back outside to the fire pit. I halfheartedly scanned the ashes for anything that might give me a clue as to what had happened here. Until recently, there had been at least seven people living in the camp. Unless Eric the zombie was somehow one of them, four were still unaccounted for.

Despite the presence of Eric's partially mutilated corpse, there was no indication that the camp had been attacked. But something had made the counselors kill themselves. They had to have known what was going on in the rest of the world. I'd seen the radio, and in the early days of the pandemic the rising number of casualties was the only thing pretty much all the stations talked about. But was that really enough to drive them to suicide?

Pushing aside the questions for now, I took the clothes inside and put them on the couch.

Next stop was the tarpaulins beside the lodge. Something furry and unnervingly large scampered away as I pulled the first of the heavy sheets back to reveal a red quad bike. I've never ridden one, but I had owned a motorcycle when I was younger, and I guessed the principles were pretty similar. Quad bikes were probably easier to ride, in fact. It was bigger than I would have expected—there was room for a couple of people on it, and it had a storage rack on the back.

The bike looked well used, one mudguard had a big dent in it, and the whole thing was scratched and spattered with dried mud. Another quad bike sat beneath the second tarpaulin. This one was blue and in slightly better condition. They both seemed to have gas in them, and I wondered how hard they were to drive. I'd seen kids on them, so presumably pretty easy. Nestled between the two bikes were four sets of ski poles and a large metal toolbox. It was rusted, and a big dent ran along one side, but the tools inside were in good condition. They'd come in very useful if I decided to stay at the camp.

I covered the bikes back up and moved around to the clearing behind the lodge. There wasn't much to it, just an expanse of grass that was beginning to get out of hand. I found a pair of tennis rackets and a couple of balls buried in the grass, none of which helped me work out what had happened to the campers. There certainly weren't any signs of a zombie attack. I'd been right about the boots: there were four pairs by the back door.

I was about to head inside when I spotted a path. The grass in the clearing was long enough that it was barely visible, but there was a definite gap in the trees, and some attempt had been made to clear away the undergrowth.

The gap led to a narrow path. Nature had begun to reclaim the trail, but I could just about make out where it wound off into the forest. It didn't occur to me not to investigate. If I was staying, I needed to know the surrounding area. And I still had the rest of the campers to find.

Chapter 7
THE PATH

Once I got into the forest a little way, the path was actually quite wide, and I made good progress. I had to push past brambles and other vegetation, but at one time there had probably been enough room for a couple of people to walk along the trail side by side.

Wooden planks formed bridges across mudholes and, at one point, a narrow stream that crossed the path. At another spot, a makeshift set of steps provided a way over a large tree. Someone had taken a wooden ladder, cut it apart, and nailed the resultant pieces to the tree trunk. It was crude, not to the quality of the camp buildings, but it was effective.

I'd been on the path for maybe ten minutes when I reached a narrow wooden bridge across a ditch. The bridge was built from three thick planks of wood. Dark moss had colonized the edges, but the upper surface was dry and wide. I didn't pay much attention to it and stepped onto the planks without thinking.

About halfway across there was a crack. The wood shifted beneath my feet, and the plank tilted sideways. I lost my balance and fell into the ditch. It wasn't deep, maybe three feet, but the fall took me by surprise. I ended up sprawled in a pile of leaves and branches. I cursed loudly.

The only casualty was my pride. I brushed a few stray twigs off my hands and stood. The ditch's sides were steep but rocky enough for me to clamber up. Near the top, I grabbed a solid-looking root protruding from ground. Muttering, I hauled myself back onto solid ground. I got to my feet and brushed the dirt off my pants. Then looked up to see a zombie coming for me.

Fumbling for my knife, I recoiled in horror, and my foot slid over the edge of the ditch. I tumbled backward. My clumsiness probably saved my life. The zombie lunged for me, and its hands brushed my face. I hit the bottom of the ditch. The impact knocked the breath from my lungs. Before I could get up, the zombie followed me over.

I rolled out of the way, and it landed half on top of me. Its face hit a rock, and its skull cracked. For a moment, I thought it had killed itself trying to get to me, but it was still moving. I struggled to get out from underneath it, but the cramped conditions made it hard to maneuver. My foot caught on a stray root. Panic welled up inside me.

The zombie's fingers wrapped around my wrist. Ragged nails sank into my flesh. I yanked my hand away, but it was as though I was chained to the thing—and the movement only pulled it closer. It made a dry, rasping sound that was part moan, part cough. A flap of skin hung loose where the rock had split its cheek. Its teeth snapped together. There was a crunch, and the corner of one tooth fell from its mouth.

I grabbed the zombie's forearm and twisted. The bones splintered, but its grip remained as tight as ever. I tried to pull myself free again. There was a tearing sound, and its wrist broke apart. With its hand still clinging to my arm, I shoved the zombie backward. It was small and light, and I had enough leverage to roll it away from me. I carried my momentum over and ended up pinning it to the ground. It twisted and snarled. Flecks of spittle and blood flew from its mouth as it fought to get at me. My heart was tearing itself out of my chest, and my hands were shaking, but there was no way it was going to get to me.

By the look of its blue overalls, the zombie had worked at the same garage as Eric. I couldn't read its name patch—it was smeared with gore—but the logo looked the same. Its face was desiccated, the skin drawn tight over high cheekbones. The few scraps of hair that still clung to its head were long and blonde. It was hard to tell for sure, but it seemed to be female.

The panic was fading now, but I was still breathing heavily. I counted to four then pulled my hunting knife from its sheath. The blade glinted in the light. I felt the shadow move as though it had been summoned by the weapon. The forest around me receded until it was just me and the zombie. I slammed the knife into the side of the zombie's head. The skull broke easily, and the knife sank to its hilt.

I felt a rush of energy. The edges of my vision turned black as the shadow started to overwhelm me. I wavered and almost fell. The world dimmed further. I clenched my fists, digging my nails into my palms. The pain was dull, but it was enough to keep me grounded in the real world. Gradually, the shadow retreated, and I regained control of my senses.

I pulled my knife from the now permanently dead zombie and stood. My legs were like jelly. I had to lean against the side of the ditch for a few minutes to stop myself from falling over again. Once I was sure I had control of my limbs, and the shadow, I clambered up to the path again.

Then I wiped the mud from my hands, took one last look at the remains of the zombie, and continued on.

A few minutes later, the trail widened, and although the forest still encroached on its edges, movement became easier. I picked up the pace. Someone had gone to a lot of trouble to make this pathway through the forest. Surely, there had to be something worthwhile at the end.

Chapter 8

ASH

That something turned out to be another cabin. The single-story building was located in the middle of a natural clearing. It was bigger than the ones in the camp, although not as big as the lodge. It had clearly been built by the same hand, but it looked much older. The walls were made from actual logs instead of cut boards, and in places bark still clung to the wood. The cabin's window frames were fitted with glass, but most of the panes were cracked. One of them was missing completely, and a flattened tin can had been used to fill the resultant hole.

Nature was wearing the building down. Moss and the odd vine grew across the roof, and its walls were slightly warped. The roof was in pretty bad shape. Dozens of shingles were missing, and it was sagging in the middle. I couldn't see any signs of life, and when I called out no one replied. The cabin's door scraped across the floor as I opened it.

"Hello?" I said, and waited.

Silence.

I stepped inside. The air was stale but laced with a faint hint of burning—smoke, ash, and charcoal.

I'd been expecting another cabin similar to those back at the camp, but it was actually a workshop. A small sink and a few cupboards took up one corner, near the back door. The rest of the room was given over to wood and metal working.

Two benches ran parallel to each other along the middle of the room. One was covered in cuts and saw marks. A sheet of metal was nailed to the surface of the second, smaller workbench. A large hacksaw lay on it, its blade dark with rust. Tables with shelves and drawers fitted beneath them lined the wall opposite the front door. All manner of tools hung on the walls—everything from simple hammers and screwdrivers to welding gear, and a metal device covered in clamps that wouldn't have looked out of place in a medieval torture chamber.

Two plastic boxes sat in one corner, filled with scraps of wood, metal bars of differing lengths, some chain, strips of leather, and two large rolls of wire. I picked through the scrap metal and wood, removed, examined, and replaced the tools, and just generally explored the workshop for a while.

Some of the wood was rotten, too far gone to be useful for anything other than firewood, but a lot was good quality. It was obviously offcuts from the construction of the camp or supplies kept handy for repairs. Likewise, most of the metal was rusty. But the wire was in good shape and plentiful enough for me to create a decent perimeter around the camp, particularly if I kept to just the lodge and a couple of the cabins.

A machete hung from a hook near the back door. It was a definite step up from the hunting knife I'd been using to defend myself so far. I considered it for a moment, thinking back to the zombie I'd bumped into in the forest, then sheathed my knife, took the machete, and continued searching the workshop. I found a shovel and placed it by the door, ready to take it back to the camp.

One set of the cupboards was full of a whole range of mechanical spare parts—carburetors, spark plugs, brake cables and pads, chains, and all manner of filters. The others held assorted nails, screws, hooks, door fittings, and hinges, all neatly sorted into mason jars. They were labeled, but the handwriting on them had faded to illegibility. There were half a dozen candles, thick and heavy with new agey names like Summer Serenity and Crystal Essence.

The back door was near the kitchen. The smell of ash and burning was stronger in that part of the workshop. When I opened the door, I realized why.

The ground behind the cabin was clear, and the remains of a fire sat in the middle of the space. The earth around it was scorched, but there wasn't much else, just a scattered jumble of blackened wood. A recently dug-over patch of ground ran along the left-hand side of the clearing, preparation for a garden perhaps. Otherwise, it was just a rectangular piece of mostly bare earth.

I watched the clearing for a few minutes, searching for signs of movement, then went outside and walked over to the remains of the fire. I kicked absentmindedly at the ash, sending a lump of wood rolling across the ground. There didn't seem to be an obvious use for the fire. Unlike the one in the camp, there was no spit for roasting food and no seats around it for late-night storytelling.

The wind picked up a little, disturbing the ash at my feet. Metal jangled quietly. It wasn't until the next gust of wind triggered another round of metallic rattles that I spotted the chain noose hanging from the branch of a pine tree at the edge of the clearing.

The chain was draped over the lowest branch, but it was still high enough that all but the tallest of people would have struggled to keep their feet on the ground while their head was in the noose. The branch was pale where the chain had scraped away the bark.

I spent a few minutes staring at the chain, trying to work out what it was for, before the answer hit me. I ran back to the fire. The chunk of wood I'd kicked was lying at the edge of the blackened circle. I knelt down and looked at it properly.

It was a lump of bone, burned almost beyond recognition. There were other charred fragments, too. The patch of ground I'd thought might be a garden was the final piece of the puzzle. I retrieved the shovel I'd found in the workshop and began to dig.

Three bodies were buried just a few inches beneath the surface. Their clothes and most of their flesh had been burned away. Two of them had broken ribs; the right arm of the third was crushed, the bones splintered. All three skulls were smashed. I was struck by the image of the camp's counselors killing their zombified charges and then trying and failing to burn the bodies. Again, I tried to feel something, sympathy maybe, but couldn't. At least now maybe I understood why they'd killed themselves. The guilt must have been overwhelming. Or perhaps they were infected themselves.

I shoveled the dirt back over the bodies. The shadow whispered to me as I worked—planting ideas in my mind, weaving together the threads until they coalesced into a plan. I turned the thoughts over in my mind, examining them from every angle, looking for flaws and finding none.

The excitement I'd felt earlier returned. The camp would provide me with shelter and some degree of safety, but the workshop? The workshop might be a place the shadow and I could resume our work.

Back inside, I took a closer look at the workbenches. They were big, well over seven feet long, and close to four feet wide. They looked as old as the rest of the workshop but well made. They'd even been bolted to the floor for good measure. I leaned into them, testing their strength. They didn't give an inch. There was lighting, too—three gas lamps hanging from the ceiling. I'd be able to work at night.

I stepped back and admired the workshop, the shadow swelling eagerly. It was perfect.

Chapter 9

GARBAGE DISPOSAL

By the time I got back to the camp, I was feeling lightheaded from lack of both water and food. I went straight to the kitchen and downed three glasses of water then dug through the cupboards and found a couple of energy bars. I'd eat properly later; for now, I just needed something to stop me from passing out.

I sat down on one of the benches near the fire pit outside the lodge. It was later than I'd thought, and the sun was high in the sky. The air was warm and muggy. I tried to remember if I'd seen any hats in the cabins. There was a lot of work to do, and I was going to be out in the open a lot of the time.

My first task was to clear the lodge of the bodies and secure it so that I had a safe place to eat and sleep. The evidence around me pointed to there being seven inhabitants of the camp. There were three bodies in the lodge and three out at the workshop. That left one unaccounted for.

I thought back to the young man I'd seen at the river the day before. Maybe he was the missing camper? I couldn't know for sure, but it didn't seem likely. He'd looked worn out, hungry, and injured. Surely, if he'd known about Camp Redfern, he'd have stayed in it rather than venturing out into the forest. Even if the bodies in the lodge made him uncomfortable, there were the other cabins. I considered them myself but in the end decided the extra space would be worth the effort.

My own attitude toward corpses is ambivalent. I don't make connections with people. In my pre-pandemic life, my job as a medical researcher had regularly brought me into contact with cadavers, but I never really saw them as human beings.

To me, a dead body is just an object—like a table or a zucchini. My motivation for getting the bodies out of the lodge had nothing to do with squeamishness. Three rotting corpses would be a health risk at best. Not from the LDN-4 virus—as far as I knew it had never gone airborne. There were other, more mundane diseases that could be just as deadly. I'd scavenged a few antibiotics and some generic pain pills, but other than that I wasn't equipped to deal with an infection.

I added *Search camp for medical kits* to my mental to-do list and finished off the energy bar, washing it down with the last of my water. Then I grabbed one of the tarpaulins from the quad bikes and took it up to the bedroom.

I started with the woman, Mary Kelson. Her body was closest to the door, and the smallest, so I figured I'd begin there and work my way up. I rolled it off the bed and onto the tarpaulin easily enough, but it took a couple of attempts to work out the best way to wrap the plastic around it. In the end, I just folded it over and dragged the whole thing across the room and down the stairs. The body made a solid *thunk thunk thunk* as it bounced from step to step.

I pulled the tarpaulin out to the front of the lodge, laying it alongside Eric the mechanic's body. Kelson was wearing baggy chinos with what seemed like an endless supply of pockets, but they were mostly empty. All I found were some crumpled up tissue and an inhaler.

I looked again at the screwdriver-shaped hole in the woman's head. In my experience, zombies could "turn" in a matter of minutes, or it could take hours. A few might stay permanently dead. I had no idea how much damage needed to be inflicted on a corpse's brain to prevent them from coming back. I'd always erred on the side of caution and done as much damage as possible. I briefly considered following the example I'd found at the workshop, and burning the bodies, but quickly decided against it. The fire pit was nearby, but I didn't know where there might be any sort of fuel, and the smoke would be visible for miles.

In the end, I dragged Kelson's body into the forest a couple of hundred yards away from the camp. I rolled it off the tarpaulin, unhooked the machete from my belt, and raised it above my head. I took a deep breath and brought the machete down on its neck. I disposed of Eric's body in the same place and decapitated it as well, just to be sure. Then I took the tarpaulin back into the lodge.

John Wrigley's body was a lot heavier than Kelson's. It took me some time to get it onto the sheet of plastic and then maneuver it outside. I searched the body and found a wallet containing a membership card for a music club, a driver's license, and a couple of credit cards. For reasons I can't really explain, I found myself wondering how much debt Wrigley had on his credit cards. I replaced the wallet and dumped the body with the others.

Back at the lodge, I stood in the bedroom, working out a strategy for getting Suter's body out as cleanly as possible. A healthy dose of blood and brains was already spattered across the floor. Even if I slept in a different room, I'd have to clean this one up, but I didn't want to make things worse if I could help it.

Flies swarmed around the body, feasting eagerly on the rotting flesh. Reaching past the corpse, I slid the window open as far as it would go, hoping the flies would sense freedom and leave. A few of them did, but most kept buzzing around the remains.

I laid out the tarpaulin behind the body then pulled the rifle from Suter's hands and placed it on the table. The chair swiveled, so I turned it around until the body was facing into the room and moved behind it.

Flies buzzed around me, grazing my face and getting caught in my hair. One landed on my lips, and I spat, grimacing and turning my head away in a futile attempt to avoid the insects. I hooked my hands under the body's arms and pushed it forward.

The chair slipped then caught on the tarpaulin. Suter's body fell forward. I let it drop the last couple of feet. As its head hit the floor, a stream of maggots burst from the hole in the back of the skull. A cloud of flies rose up into the air. I swatted at them, directing them toward the window. They swarmed around me, bumping into my face and chest. I felt one crawling on my ear and shook my head, waving a hand at it and hoping I wasn't encouraging it to hide in my ear canal.

Slowly, the flies dispersed. A lot of them returned to the body, but a few zigzagged out the window and were gone. The rest swept around the room, crashing into walls or crawling over the furniture. They seemed so mindless, I wondered if perhaps they'd died and become "zomflies." Trying to ignore them, I rolled the body up in the tarpaulin and dragged it out of the room.

The flies buzzed and whirred as I dragged the body down the stairs. Each bump dislodged a few more, and I left behind a trail of maggots. As soon as I got the body outside and away from the lodge, I opened up the tarpaulin to let the flies out. This time, most of them did fly away, sailing off into the clear blue skies. I kicked the body a few times to rouse more of them then rolled it back up and dragged it to where I dumped the other corpses, leaving the tarpaulin behind this time.

It took me a couple of hours and what felt like dozens of buckets of bloodied water to clean the room. Thankfully, most of Suter's remains had ended up on the rug, and I dumped that in the forest. The floor was still stained in places when I'd finished, but the room no longer looked like an abattoir. Some concerted spraying of air freshener replaced the smell of blood and decay with a subtle pine scent.

The effort of cleaning up had made me hungry and lightheaded. I headed back inside, drank some more water, and made myself a meal of carrots, apples, and peanut butter. It wasn't exactly a feast, and I savored it as best I could, but it was gone all too quickly. Resisting the temptation to eat more, I sat on the couch, my eyelids drifting closed as sleep tried to claim me.

My chin hit my chest, and I snapped awake. The lodge was getting dark. I stood, and the blood rushed to my head. I waited with my eyes closed for a moment until I'd stopped swaying. Plate in hand, I checked the doors and windows on my way to the kitchen. I checked them again on the way back.

I grabbed my backpack and then paused at the bottom of the stairs, gazing up into the darkness. I knew the rooms were empty, but even without the bodies something made me hesitant to spend the night up there.

That ancient part of me, the part that was still afraid of the dark, wanted nothing to do with the suicides. My hand found the machete still hanging from my belt. I'd left my flashlight somewhere, but I was armed. I could lock the door. I had nothing to be afraid of. The shadow urged me forward, silencing that ancient voice.

With my hand still on the machete, I climbed the stairs and entered the first room. The clothes were still scattered across the floor. I halfheartedly moved some of them out of the way and retrieved the pillow from the corner of the room, but the real cleanup operation would have to wait until the morning.

The moonlight coming in through the window was strong enough for me to check the wardrobe and under the bed. The room was still empty. I swung the door shut and locked it then checked the room one last time before I lay down. I was asleep by the time my head hit the pillow.

Chapter 10

PREPARATIONS

I woke with the thick taste of blood in my mouth. The vision of a zombie lunging at me filled my mind. I panicked, sat upright, and kicked out at the imagined horror. My heart was hammering in my chest, nineteen to the dozen as my mother would have said. I could taste blood on my tongue. I wiped my sweat-slick hands on the sheets and fought to regain some measure of control.

The intellectual part of my brain, the part I relied on to keep me alive, gradually reasserted control.

I was in the lodge.

There were no zombies.

I took eight deep breaths, counting to four on each inhale and again on the exhale. My heart slowed. I dabbed at my lip and winced. My fingers came away wet with blood. I'd bitten it, and it was puffy and tender.

It was still early, but the room was bathed in a warm yellow glow. My arms and legs ached dully after my exertions the day before. Despite that, there was no chance I'd get back to sleep. My mind was already whirring. A dozen questions competed for my attention. Did anyone else know about the camp? Could I make my home here? Where was the last inhabitant? Were they trapped somewhere in the camp, a zombie?

I gave up trying to sleep, dressed, and went downstairs. After a meal of a discount-brand breakfast bar and the last of the aging fruit, I decided to start the day by assessing what supplies I had.

If I wanted to make the lodge my base of operations, my sanctuary within a sanctuary, then I needed everything close at hand. I emptied the kitchen cupboards and placed the contents on the table in the center of the room. Then I went through the rest of the lodge and all four cabins, loading up with anything remotely useful and transporting it back to the kitchen. I tidied up my room as well, dumping all of the clothes into the pink suitcase and cramming it shut.

When I'd collected everything, I admired my haul. There was a lot less food than I'd hoped. Most of it had been in the kitchen, although there were half a dozen cans of energy drink and several boxes of protein bars stashed in the graffiti cabin.

There were two camping stoves and four spare propane bottles, so at least I'd be able to eat some hot food. If I was careful, there were maybe a couple of months of soups, chili, instant noodles, canned vegetables, and crackers, along with some cartons of fruit juice.

I was vaguely disappointed that I didn't find any alcohol, but after the scene outside the workshop, I wasn't really surprised. If there's ever a time for Dutch courage, it's when you're about to kill and cremate your once-human, now-zombified friends.

The cabins had yielded plenty of clothes, including a lot

that would fit me well enough. I'd loaded up the biggest of the seven suitcases with anything I'd feel comfortable wearing and put it in my room.

Beyond the food and clothes, I'd gathered a generous collection of medical supplies including a small first aid kit in a green plastic case, painkillers, bandages, disinfectant, and various lotions for bites and sunburn. I'd found a bottle of antibiotics in the psychedelic cabin, but there were only a few tablets left. I combined them with the few I already had. I'd also discovered some climbing rope beneath one of the beds. The ends were frayed, but otherwise, it seemed in good condition.

Weapons were few and far between. Other than the rifle Suter had used to blow his brains out, there were no guns and only a couple of hunting knives. I found a box of bullets for the rifle high up on a shelf in the kitchen. There were about thirty rounds, .270s according to the box. I'd never fired a gun and didn't like the idea of advertising my presence by practicing, but it would come in useful in an emergency or to discourage the living from causing trouble.

The knives were in better condition than mine, but they were smaller and probably less effective, so I put them to one side. I'd have to check the workshop for a sharpening stone next time I was out there.

There were a dozen or so books, mostly trashy popular fiction. But there were some on local flora and fauna, an English-French dictionary, and a battered paperback of Stephen King's *The Stand*. I put that one aside and stacked the rest on the table in the lounge.

I'd found a photo album, too, containing twenty years of captured Camp Redfern memories. I flicked through it, but there was nothing other than the usual banal campsite scenes.

The rest of the scavenged items were largely useless—keys, tourist mementos, things like that. But there was a hand-drawn map of the surrounding area. I found it sandwiched between two hardcover books on trees. It was almost three feet square and had obviously been created over the years by successive visitors to the camp. An intricate banner ran along the top, proclaiming it to be "A Visitors Guide to Camp Redfern and the Surrounding Environs."

It covered an extensive area, at least sixteen square miles according to the measurements written along its sides. The camp was at the center, and the map had expanded from there over time as numerous artists added landmarks, natural features, and the sites of events that were significant in the camp's history. There were a few places I recognized —the river, the road where I'd found the broken-down truck, a logging trail, and the workshop. The distances to each landmark were labeled, and the numbers seemed fairly accurate, at least for the locations I knew.

The map also showed a ranger station twenty or so miles upriver. I wondered if that was where the military had made their base. If it was, having them that close was a mark against the camp. There was also a lake someone had christened Camel, presumably because of its twin-humped shape, a ridge that had been the site of the Great Water Fight of 2010, and most interestingly, a cluster of buildings marked Sally's Home Comforts. Someone had recently drawn a crude knife, fork, and bottle next to the buildings in case there was any question what home comforts Sally might be willing to provide.

I carefully folded the map up and put it in the dining room with the books. It was really quite impressive, a work of art in some ways. It would also be very useful if I was going to live in the camp for any length of time.

Once I'd sorted through everything and filled the kitchen cupboards with the food and medical supplies, it was lunchtime. I opted for a protein bar and some of the dried fruit. The bar was powdery and had an antiseptic taste. I wished I'd taken the time to warm up some soup.

My thoughts turned to the workshop. In my head, it was perfect for my purposes. Near enough to the camp that I could move between the two quickly, but not so close that you'd see it from the lodge. The two benches were solid and stable. Once I'd made a few modifications, it would be an ideal place for me to work. And the tools? They'd open up new possibilities, vistas I'd never dreamed of in my closeted existence in the city. I could sense the shadow's excitement.

It was perfect. Too perfect.

My subconscious gnawed at me. There had to be something wrong with it. The location was more exposed than I'd imagined, or the cabin had been less secure. I hadn't noticed a road that ran nearby, or that it was on a direct path to the ranger station. Maybe someone was even living there and I'd been too blind to notice the signs. My fears wore me down, made me tired and irritable. I needed to go back to the workshop and check, to prepare things. Then I could relax and make my plans.

I dug through my backpack, removing the random assortment of tape, tools, and books that had gotten me through the weeks since I'd left the city. I filled up a couple of water bottles and added them to the pack, begrudgingly including some jerky.

After some internal debate, I decided to leave the rifle behind. Not that I was afraid of killing, of course. But a rifle was too distant, too impersonal for my liking, and my lack of skill would provide ample opportunity for attackers to disarm me before I got a shot off. I decided to stick with the machete.

Finally, I picked up the battered rectangular leather case that held my most prized possessions. An oval metal plate was mounted on the lid, and I stroked it, idly. In some ways, I was loath to take it with me.

I had visions of my pack tearing on a stray branch and the case falling out without my realizing or any number of other nightmarish scenarios. But leaving it behind was worse. What if someone came to the camp? I still hadn't accounted for all the inhabitants, and there was no telling who else was wandering the forest. And that was ignoring the ever-present threat of the military or other survivors. An inquisitive pilot might notice signs of my presence and come to investigate.

No, I'd take the case with me.

I slipped it into the backpack, pushing it right down to the bottom so that I wasn't likely to pull it out accidentally. I put away the rest of the supplies, checked the case was still safe inside the backpack, then headed out.

***

The journey to the workshop was uneventful, but it took longer than I remembered. The trail seemed to stretch out endlessly in front of me. Several times I became concerned that I'd strayed off the path and missed the workshop, dooming me to hours of fruitless wandering until I passed out from hunger or was found by the dozens of zombies that must surely be nearby. My concerns eased when I reached the ditch I'd fallen in and saw the body still lying there, the hole where my knife had penetrated its skull clearly visible.

I grew more and more nervous as I approached the

workshop. All manner of disastrous scenarios played out in my head—everything from a swarm of zombies surrounding the cabin to it having been burned down by a roving post-apocalyptic gang. No matter what I said to myself, I couldn't shake the feeling that my plan was going to unravel around me before it even started.

In the end, I needn't have worried. The workshop was largely how I remembered it. It was perhaps a little smaller, and not every tool I thought I'd seen was actually there, but there were no signs of visitors beyond the trail of dusty footprints I'd left behind myself.

I set my pack on the floor, pulled out a bottle of water, and took a few sips as I walked around the workshop, mentally noting the various tools on the walls. It was doubtful that I'd use most of them. They were too crude and imprecise for my purposes, but I'd need some basics to make my improvements to the workbenches.

Searching through the drawers, I found some U-shaped brackets. I removed six, picked out some screws that would fit them, along with a box of heavy-duty bolts, a hand-operated drill, and a screwdriver. I placed everything on the larger of the two workbenches and then dug around in the plastic boxes and found three lengths of chain.

An hour later, I'd fitted the chains to the table. One end of each of them was securely bolted to the side of the workbench. The other end was loose but could be fastened to the opposite side of the bench by running it through the brackets and pulling it tight. I'd use three more bolts to lock the chains in position.

I pulled on each chain in turn, getting my full weight behind them in an effort to dislodge them. They seemed solid enough. I tried to move the workbenches again, but they didn't budge.

After another walk around the workshop, I was convinced everything seemed secure. I wasn't completely happy with the number of tools—and therefore the number of makeshift weapons—but I doubted my subjects were going to be in any shape to use them. I did clear a space around both of the workbenches, making sure anything that could be used as a weapon was out of reach.

Finally, I pulled the leather case out of my backpack. I tapped my fingers against the lid as I debated what to do with it. If I left it in the workshop, it would be close at hand, and probably safer than at the camp, but there were fewer places to hide it. If someone did find the workshop and chose to search it, they were bound to find the case.

I bounced back and forth for several minutes. In the end, I found the deepest, fullest drawer and put the case at the back of it. I pushed the drawer's contents around and added piles of loose screws and bits of wire until it was packed full of junk. Nerves twisted my stomach as I closed the drawer again.

It took four circuits of the room before I was satisfied I had a clear picture of the workshop and that my subconscious wouldn't be able to taunt me with misremembered details.

I tightened the bolts holding the chains in place and gave them one last pull, then I went outside. I walked slowly around the cabin, trying to imprint the building and its surroundings on my memory. A generator sat against one wall. It was similar to the one at the lodge but smaller. If the fuel gauge was accurate, there was about a third of a tank of gas left.

The workshop doors weren't fitted with locks, and I added a padlock to the list of supplies I needed. I picked up a couple of thin twigs and propped them against each door.

At least then I'd have some indication as to whether I'd had visitors while I was away.

As sure as I could be that the workshop was secure, I headed back to the lodge. It was early, but I needed to get some rest. My arms and legs ached, and I had a big day coming up.

Chapter 11

HUNTING TRIP

I set out early the next morning, heading west along the wider road out of the camp. I had my backpack with me, stocked with enough food and water for a full day's hiking, although I hoped I wouldn't need it all. I took the climbing rope with me as well. The end was tied into a lasso big enough to fit around a human. I also had the machete, just in case things didn't go according to plan.

The track wound through the forest, rising and falling for a mile or so before joining a bigger logging road. I went south toward more populated areas, figuring that gave me a better chance of finding what I was looking for—a zombie.

The forest was warm and muggy, and the sky was filled with low clouds that promised rain. I was wearing two coats —a thick leather jacket belonging to either Arlo Chan or his roommate and my own hunting jacket over the top. They were heavy and far too hot in the oppressive atmosphere, but I figured they'd give me at least some degree of protection from teeth.

I trudged along, slowly cooking in my own sweat. Another trail joined the logging road. The trail was wide enough for a single vehicle, and by the look of the ruts in the ground it was well used. On a whim, I turned onto it, still heading south.

Within a few minutes, I spotted a logging camp up ahead. I slowed and moved to the edge of the trail. The camp was small with just a single tent, a generator, and a couple of sawhorses. I ducked into the trees. I'd found a zombie.

The man was shirtless. In life, he would have been solidly built—muscular and strong. In death, the muscles beneath the zombie's skin had begun to decay, giving it an oddly soft shape. A split cut across its back. The gash's edges were green and weeping. It was standing in the middle of the camp, barely moving.

I unhooked the rope from my belt and crouched in the trees for a while, watching the zombie. If it sensed me, it didn't respond. As the seconds passed, the shadow rose within me, and my excitement rose with it. A smile formed on my lips, almost involuntarily. The shadow quickly grew more confident as it realized I was letting it out to play. I could feel the rope in my hands, warm and eager to be put to good use. I had to force myself not to move too hastily, not to get overexcited.

Eventually, the shadow's insistent whispers became too much to ignore. Without taking my eyes off the zombie, I slipped my backpack off and quietly placed it on the ground. When the zombie didn't respond, I coiled up the rope and walked slowly out of the trees. A quiet calm descended over me.

I got as close as I dared before stopping and uncoiling the rope. There was a moment of doubt, a brief flash of concern as I realized I should have practiced with the lasso. Now that I was actually here, it seemed foolish to think I could just go and rope myself a zombie like some post-apocalyptic Clint Eastwood.

I let the concerns drift over me. I wasn't on a horse; my target wasn't a galloping stallion. The loop I'd made for the lasso was big, and the zombie wasn't even moving. This was more like tossing a hoop over a bottle at a funfair but without the game being fixed. I was only about ten feet away from the zombie, and it was still in a near-catatonic state. At this rate, I could just walk up to it and drop the rope over its head.

The wind rustled through the trees, and I glanced up at the sky. The clouds were still thick, gray, and threatening rain. I needed to hurry up.

I shook the lasso four times to work out the kinks then took the end of the rope in my left hand, the loop in my right. I had no intention of whirling it around my head or trying any other theatrics. Instead, I just flicked the rope forward and released the loop. It sailed through the air and flopped over the zombie's head. One side of the lasso caught on the thing's shoulder for a moment, but then it came loose. It fell to the zombie's waist, trapping its arms. I pulled, and it felt as though I'd wrapped the rope around a tree and was now trying to drag it away. I tugged again, tightening the rope as far as it would go.

Finally, the zombie moved.

Its head whipped around. Its black, soulless eyes fixed on me. I tightened my grip on the rope. The zombie's mouth opened, revealing bloodstained teeth. It let out a loud, gravelly roar and then sprinted toward me.

I let go of the rope, turned, and ran.

I'd barely taken four steps when another zombie loomed up out of the forest to my right. This one was wearing a shirt, but if anything the clothing just made it look bigger and more dangerous. Its right hand was mangled, a crushed and bloodied stump. The creature moaned as it broke through the bushes.

I dodged left. My feet skidded on the soft earth. I stumbled forward. My hands hit the ground, and I barely managed to keep myself upright as my momentum tried to send me sprawling.

Something moaned behind me. The sound was so close I could almost feel the zombie's rancid breath on my neck. Adrenaline surged through me.

As I reached the edge of the camp, a third zombie appeared out of the undergrowth. This one was a woman. It was much shorter than me, close to five feet tall, and with a thin, wiry physique. Whereas the two men had been largely intact, the woman's throat had been partially torn out, and there were long slashes down its face. There were shotgun wounds in its left shoulder and chest, and a knife protruded from its right thigh.

It staggered across the trail, the injuries making its movements uneven. Instinctively, I slowed to avoid running into it. Something big and heavy hit me from behind. For an instant, I thought I'd been run over by a truck or maybe a low-flying aircraft. I was flung forward, toward the woman.

I tried to tuck and roll, but my legs got tangled up in each other. I went sprawling across the ground. The impact sent a jarring pain up my arm and into my shoulder. I rolled in what I hoped was the opposite direction to the zombies and then flipped onto my back.

The first zombie had run into me. The fact that its arms were still trapped at its side by the lasso had probably saved my life. If it had been able to grab me, it would have sunk its teeth into my neck before I could react. It lunged toward me, mouth open and dripping a viscous black fluid. I reached for my machete, spending a few heart-stopping seconds searching for it before my fingers wrapped around the hilt.

The zombie fell on top of me. The impact cracked my head against the hard ground and knocked the wind from my lungs. Blackness seeped around the edges of my vision. The zombie reared up in front of me, its gray skin stretched taut across the sharp bones of its skull. I lifted my arm as it attacked, and its jaw fastened around my forearm. Its teeth felt like razor blades, and I screamed as it chewed at my arm. I swung the machete in one last, desperate attempt at survival.

I felt the blade sink into flesh and connect with bone. I'd hit the creature's neck. It wasn't enough to kill it, but it loosened its grip on my arm. I pushed the machete away from me, trying to force the zombie backward. It was too heavy and barely moved. I struggled sideways and managed to partly free myself. My legs were still pinned beneath the creature, but my upper body was free. It snarled and spat as I yanked the machete from its throat and attacked again.

This time, my aim was better. I jammed the machete up through its jaw. Black fluid burst from the wound, soaking my hands and splattering my face. A putrid stench washed over me, and I found myself fighting for air. It let out a strangled, wordless cry then collapsed. Dead again.

My arm was covered in blood, but it was thick and black and belonged to the zombie I'd just killed. The jackets had protected me. I muttered a quiet prayer of thanks that I'd put up with the heat rather than discarding the extra layers.

I dragged myself from beneath the corpse and pushed myself upright onto wavering legs just in time to face the second zombie. It charged toward me. These zombies were moving so much faster than the others I'd encountered. I held the machete out in front of me, at about head height.

The zombie ran straight into it.

The blade's point sank into its eye. The impact knocked me backward. What little sense I had left made me let go of the machete and throw myself sideways, out of its path. It barreled past me and continued for five or six steps before collapsing to the ground. The fall drove the machete deeper until its silver tip protruded from the back of the zombie's skull. I grabbed the machete's handle and pulled, but it was wedged tight.

The female zombie was slower than the men, perhaps because of the extent of its injuries, but I could see it bearing down on me as I struggled to free the machete. I didn't have long. Reluctant to lose my weapon, I tried to twist it free. It held firm, and with the female zombie almost on top of me, I gave up.

Cursing at my stupidity, I ran down the trail, away from the logging camp.

Chapter 12

REGRETS

I sat at the table in the lodge's kitchen with my head in my hands. Partly it was out of despair, partly to stop them shaking. I was an idiot. I'd been unprepared, careless. I was lucky to get away alive. My hunting jacket was lying on the ground outside the lodge where I'd thrown it in frustration. Despite the protection of the leather jacket, my forearm was bruised and sore. It was a wonder the zombie hadn't managed to break any bones. To add insult to injury, I'd left the rope, my backpack, and the machete behind. And there was no way I was going back to get them.

Panic hit me—my case. I thought I remembered putting it in the drawer in the workshop, but had I dreamed that? Was the case still in the pack, out in the forest? I clenched the table and closed my eyes.

No, I could see the drawer and the junk I'd used to hide the case. It was safe. I ignored the voice whispering in my ear insisting that someone had broken into the workshop.

I took four deep breaths and focused on what to do next. Part of me was convinced I should give up and concentrate on surviving, not indulging the shadow's desires. No matter how keenly I felt its influence, if I let it control my decisions, it would be my downfall.

But another part of me was convinced I couldn't let an opportunity like this slip through my fingers. I don't believe in a deity, benevolent or otherwise, but if I did, my discovery of the camp and the workshop could be interpreted as a sign that I had waited long enough. It was time to unleash the shadow again.

Yes, I'd been careless, and yes, I hadn't prepared, but I had survived. It seemed not all zombies were created equal. These, the two men at least, had been quicker and stronger than any I'd seen. But I'd gone up against them and gotten away with my life.

I wasn't willing to abandon my plan. Overall, it was a good one. It was my execution that had been lacking. With the benefit of hindsight, I could see exactly where I'd gone wrong. I'd let my excitement and the influence of the shadow overwhelm my judgment. It wouldn't happen again.

The rope had also been a bad idea. I'd envisaged myself pulling the zombie along behind me as I traveled through the forest, treating it like some sort of oversize dog. My pace would prevent it from attacking me. If it did stray too close, a tug on the rope would knock it off balance and enable me to keep out of the way. At least, that had been the idea.

Clearly, that wouldn't be good enough. I had some rope left, but I needed something that would let me hold the zombie at a safe distance while we made our way through the forest.

I must have spent at least an hour sitting at the kitchen table, considering and discarding ever more ludicrous ideas before I saw the broom leaning up against the wall. The pieces clicked into place. I grabbed the broom, kicked off the head, and brought it over to the table. I measured the rope against the width of the broom handle, and a smile spread over my face. I could drill a couple holes in the handle, feed the rope through it, and create a noose. It would act like a sort of zombie snare. Once I'd gotten it around a zombie's neck, I'd be able to control its movements using the broom handle.

My problem was solved.

It took me almost three hours to get to the workshop, drill the required holes, and create the snare. I tested it multiple times around the back of the workshop, using a branch on a tree to represent my prey. The noose worked perfectly. It wouldn't be enough to hold a big zombie like the ones I'd found at the logging camp, but from now on I'd stick to weaker subjects. Put like that, it makes me sound like a coward, but I prefer to think of it as a healthy reaction to the close proximity of death's bony hand.

By the time I'd finished and I was sure my new weapon would work, it was getting late. Part of me wanted to go out anyway, but I knew that was stupid. Even if I bumped into a suitable subject, it was going to take me a while to get them back to the workshop. I didn't fancy trailing through the forest in the dark with a slavering zombie in tow.

As I walked to the lodge, I convinced myself I was being smart by waiting, not a coward.

The shadow stirred, but I quashed it.

"Tomorrow," I said. "Tomorrow, I'll get it right."

Chapter 13

SNARED

I headed west again, following the same route as the day before. I'd found another backpack, this one red, and had felt a burst of frustration as I'd put a couple of protein bars and a bottle of water into it. I couldn't afford to keep wasting this much food.

When I reached the point where I'd turned south down the path that led me to the camp, I carried on along the wider logging road. I checked the path as I passed. It was clear of zombies, but I still didn't want to risk trying to get my pack. Maybe some other time.

The previous day's clouds had broken without depositing their rain on the forest. The sky was clear apart from a few scraps of white that would soon burn off. It was still early and not too hot, but in a couple of hours that would change.

A few minutes down the logging road, I paused to take a drink. An insect buzzed past my ear, and somewhere off in the distance a bird cried out. I've never been one for hiking or other outdoor activities, but standing there in the sun, with the forest coming to life around me, I could at least understand the appeal.

As I put my bottle of water away, there was a snap. It was the sound of wood breaking. Across from me, twenty feet or so into the forest, was a zombie. I crouched down then maneuvered off the road and behind a nearby tree.

The zombie was a short, thin young man with bright blond hair. It was wearing shorts and a basketball jersey, both of which were about three times too big for it. Its back was twisted as though suffering from some sort of spinal injury. Its neck was broken, too, and its head tilted downward, looking at its feet. That was probably why it hadn't seen me. I watched as it approached the road, annoyed at myself for not seeing it sooner.

I could hear it moaning. Every time it placed its right foot on the ground, it let out a short grunt as though putting weight on that foot hurt. The zombie stumbled a couple of times, eliciting more moans, but otherwise, it just kept moving relentlessly forward. It was completely oblivious to me and the rest of the world.

I moved out of the zombie's path, keeping a careful eye on the forest around me in case it wasn't alone. It stepped onto the road, and I got ready to run if it saw me. It didn't. It just plodded on.

As I'd suspected, its spine was damaged. I could see pale splinters of bone protruding through the shirt from three different places. How it managed to stay upright, I couldn't tell you. Other than that and a general appearance of overall decay, the zombie was relatively intact. It didn't even smell that bad yet.

My anxiety grew, but it brought the shadow with it. Slow-moving, small, and not particularly muscular, the zombie was exactly what I was looking for.

I shook out the snare at the end of the broom, loosening the rope until it was big enough for me to get over the zombie's head without too much difficulty. I circled around behind it, alert to any sign that it had noticed me. It shambled on, apparently still oblivious to my presence. My hands felt hot and sticky. I took a deep breath and closed my eyes, willing my racing heart to slow before it tore itself from its mounts.

The zombie was three-quarters of the way across the road now, and despite its steady pace, there was a danger it would reach the forest before I could catch it. If it did that, my task would be that much harder—and harder was not something I needed. I took another deep breath, counted to four, and stalked after the zombie.

I raised the snare. The wooden broom handle was unexpectedly unwieldy. The circle of rope wavered in the air. The zombie let out an agitated groan. I let it take four more steps forward then dropped the noose over its head.

The zombie moaned and turned toward me. I pulled the rope to tighten the noose. It caught on the zombie's chin, and I felt things slipping out of control again. I loosened the snare, just a fraction, and shook it.

Now that it was facing me, the zombie had finally realized I was there, and it let out a loud groan. The rope flipped upward and landed in its mouth. I flicked the broom handle again, and this time the rope came loose and dropped around the zombie's neck. I pulled it tight.

The zombie bucked and twisted, trying to free itself. I braced my feet. Then it took another uneven step toward me. I responded by pushing back with the broom handle. It stumbled backward. Excitement took the place of my anxiety. It was working. The rope still had some give in it, and the broom handle wasn't as long as I'd have liked, but it was really working.

Now I just had to get it back to the workshop.

I tugged at the broom handle, giving the zombie a little encouragement. It let out a soft groan and stumbled toward me. Every time it took a step, I took one of my own, keeping the distance between me and the creature consistent.

Slowly, I backed down the path. The ground was uneven beneath my feet. Under normal circumstances, it wouldn't have been enough to cause me any difficulties, but with a zombie in tow, each ridge and rock became a potentially fatal hazard. And I had to keep an eye out for other zombies as well.

This was going to take a while.

I adjusted the noose's position a couple of times, trying to find a way to hold it comfortably, move quickly, and still keep the zombie at bay. In the end, I had to content myself with moving sideways, crab-like. That way, I could look ahead at where I was going and keep an eye on the zombie. Every couple of minutes I swapped sides to stop anything creeping up behind me.

It was slow going, and by the time I got within sight of the camp, the sun was high in the sky, and sweat was running down my back. I could feel heat baking into my skin. I hadn't dared stop to drink or eat since I'd snared the zombie, but I still had to get to the workshop.

Distracted by thoughts of water and sunblock, I caught my foot on a tree root and fell. I hit the ground, and a thick branch stuck into the soft flesh of my thigh.

The zombie staggered forward, a gargling rumble forming in its throat. The broom handle slipped out of my hand and bounced across the ground away from me. The zombie lumbered closer, its jaw dropping open. The subtle smell of mold and death I'd caught from it earlier was stronger now, accentuated by the heat of the midday sun. I twisted to my right, lashing out with my feet and hoping to connect with the zombie's shins and at least slow it down.

I missed.

I rolled across the trail, four complete revolutions that covered me in dirt and leaves but put several valuable feet between me and the creature. It stumbled after me. It was hunched over, arms stretched out. Under different circumstances, the sight would have been comical.

I ran out of room to roll and struggled to my feet. Blood rushed to my head, and a wave of dizziness washed over me. The world blurred, and my legs buckled, threatening to dump me back on the ground. I bent over, mirroring the zombie's pose, and again I was struck by just how ridiculous this would look to someone not in harm's way.

The blood stopped rushing to my head, and the world came back into focus. I backed away from the zombie, moving up the trail toward the camp. Worst-case scenario: I could run and take cover in the lodge. The zombie turned to face me, its head flopping on its broken neck. It was dragging the snare along behind it now. The handle was well out of my reach, but I was back on my feet and surely quick enough to escape—if I stayed calm.

Something snapped behind me. I whirled around, scanning the forest for movement, but the trees were too thick. I couldn't see more than a few feet beyond the edge of the path.

The zombie let out a gurgling cry and took three quick steps toward me. I was almost ready to declare my plan a lost cause and run.

The shadow wormed its way into my consciousness. It fought against my fear, bringing with it a grim determination. Letting out a cry of rage, I ran at the zombie. I curved around it in an arc that kept me out of reach of its clutching arms. As I ran past, I scooped up the broom handle. The slick wood slipped through my fingers, and I almost lost my grip. Almost but not quite.

I rammed the broom handle at the zombie's face. The noose had gone slack, but the handle caught its jaw and forced it backward. It let out a snarl of frustration. I jabbed with the broom handle again, this time hitting it in the shoulder. The trailing end of the noose was lying on the ground nearby. While the zombie was off balance, I grabbed the rope and pulled. The noose slid tight around its neck again.

The zombie pushed forward, trying to get at me. I stood firm, the broom handle held out before me, keeping the creature at a safe distance while my heart slowed and the adrenaline coursing through my system faded to more reasonable levels. Once they had and I was convinced everything was under control again, I circled carefully around the zombie and continued along the trail.

I approached the camp slowly, looking for any indication that someone had discovered my sanctuary. I doubted I was the only living being in the forest, and I didn't want to have to explain what I was doing traipsing around with a zombie in tow. Everything looked as I had left it, but I waited outside the camp for a few minutes anyway before leading the zombie around the lodge toward the trail to the workshop.

Once I was on the trail, I felt a lot more comfortable. My thigh was sore where the branch had stuck it when I fell, and somewhere along the line I'd grazed the knuckles on my right hand. But the trees provided shelter from the oppressive heat, I knew where I was going, and I was getting the hang of crabbing my way along. The zombie lumbered after me with very little encouragement, its carnivorous instincts more than sufficient to keep it moving as though I were a man-size carrot dangling from a stick attached to its head.

About halfway to the workshop, I heard the familiar *whump-whump-whump* of a helicopter. I searched the forest for a place we could hide, but there was nowhere suitable. Trying to lead the zombie off the trail would just be asking for trouble.

The sound of the helicopter grew louder. I ducked my head slightly in a worthless attempt at concealment. The zombie moaned and strained against the noose. I shoved at it with the broom. Its groans grew louder. I flinched as though the helicopter's pilot might somehow hear the sound.

The helicopter roared past, close but still not visible. As the sound faded away, I felt my shoulders relax, and let out the breath I'd been holding.

I straightened the broom handle and got a better grip that wouldn't slip free. Then I moved along the trail as fast as I could, leading the zombie toward the workshop.

Chapter 14
THE SHADOW

The building was as I'd left it. I checked the twigs I'd leaned against the front doors, and it didn't seem like anyone had been inside while I was away. Unless they'd seen me put the twigs in place and replaced them after they'd entered the cabin. Or maybe they were just waiting somewhere beyond the tree line to come out, guns blazing, as soon as I was looking the other way.

I didn't have time to worry about it. My arms were tired from dragging the zombie around, and I still hadn't had anything to eat or drink. I pushed open the door to the workshop, took a quick look around to make sure there was nothing out of place, and then dragged the zombie inside.

As I led it toward the workbench, I felt the shadow wake. A warm burst of energy shot through me, restoring life to my tired limbs.

Forcing some small degree of caution into my actions, I maneuvered the zombie until it was standing with its back to one end of the table. It snarled at me, teeth clacking, black eyes locked on to my throat. I raised the broomstick until the snare was level with its neck and pushed. The zombie leaned back then started to struggle. The rope dug into its flesh as it fought against me. Somewhere, a bone snapped. I gave the handle another shove, hoping to unbalance the creature, but it was too strong, and I barely made any impact. The rope cut into its neck. A scrap of flesh fell to the floor.

A tiny nugget of doubt formed at the back of my mind, but the shadow rose up, smothering it before it could take root. I rammed the broomstick forward, driving the zombie as far back as I could, then let go and dived toward its legs. Before common sense could dissuade me, I wrapped my arms around its calves and lifted.

The snare bounced across the workshop floor. The zombie let out a desperate growl. It tipped backward, its head slamming into the table with a heavy thunk. I let go and circled around the table, grabbing the broom as I passed. I pulled on the handle, dragging the zombie down as it tried to sit up. I shouted at it, a wordless scream equal parts excitement and fear.

The zombie's head rolled backward, dead eyes searching. As soon as it saw me, it reached toward my face. Its arms flailed in the air. Praying I wasn't about to tear the creature's head right off, I backed away from the table, dragging it by the neck. It clawed at the rope around its throat—it still had enough intelligence to realize it needed to free itself from my snare. The noose sank into its flesh. Its groans turned to wet, gargling coughs.

I dragged the creature across the table until its head was almost at the edge then dropped the broom handle and lunged toward the chains. Its moans grew more insistent as it lost sight of me. I grabbed the first chain, threw it across its neck, and ran to the other side of the table.

The zombie spotted me and reached out as I passed. Its

fingers caught my jacket. A surge of terror swept over me. I twisted out of its grip, almost tripping over my own feet. The chain rattled as the creature began to sit up. I grabbed the end and pulled, forcing it back down onto the workbench. It groaned and swiped at me, but I was out of its reach.

I threaded the chain through the brackets and pulled it as tight as I could. Confidence surged through me as I slid the bolt through the chain. The zombie tried to sit up again, but the chain held. Black blood seeped from its neck where the chain held it down.

The zombie kicked out and almost slid off the table. I grabbed its legs, hauling them back onto the bench and wrapping the second chain around them. It kicked again as I pulled the chain through the brackets. It almost managed to work itself free, but I got the chain tightened and locked just in time.

The zombie was tied down now, but I secured the third chain across its waist, just to be sure. It kicked and thrashed. The chains rattled but held.

I circled around the workbench, my movements slow and deliberate. The shadow filled me. It brought with it a sense of calm. I could feel it pressing against my skin, eager to burst forth. My hunger, my thirst, my fears of infection and death evaporated. They were nothing. Neurons fired deep within my brain. Possibilities opened up in front of me, flashes of dark genius that fed the shadow, drove its desires.

This was the shadow's time.

This was my destiny.

When I reached the bench's head, I slipped the backpack off my shoulder and placed it on the floor. I retrieved some scissors from a pegboard on the wall and cut away the zombie's basketball jersey to expose its chest. Its skin was gray and stretched tight across its ribs. It made a halfhearted attempt to free itself then dropped its head back to the bench.

I replaced the scissors then opened the drawer containing my tool kit. My fingers were immediately drawn to the case, and a tingle of excitement rippled through me as they brushed against the soft leather. I pulled it from the drawer. Time slowed.

The zombie grew still. It was lying there watching me as I delicately unclipped the brass catch and opened the lid. Five scalpels lay inside, along with six replacement blades still wrapped in semitransparent paper. I ran my fingers over the scalpels, savoring the touch of the cold metal. I closed my eyes and let the shadow guide me until my fingers came to rest on the second one from the left. The scalpel popped free with the barest pressure. I weighed it in my hand for a moment.

A quiet calm descended over me. The cacophonous world, the myriad of banal thoughts that normally battered my senses, dropped away until all that was left was the zombie lying on the table.

My subject.

My victim.

The shadow flowed through me and revealed the zombie's true form. Black, oily ribbons of guilt grew from deep within its chest. They drifted in the air like seaweed floating on the current. A deep cut in the man's side revealed a spiderweb of black fibers woven through the gray flesh. Corrupted blood seeped from the wound. It pooled around its body, thickening and becoming a lake of obsidian guilt.

I pressed my hand against the zombie's chest, seeking out the perfect point for the first incision. I found it just above its heart and placed the scalpel's tip against its skin. Black veins exploded outward and spread across its body. Its skin tightened, crackling. Dark pustules erupted across the zombie's face as the guilt bubbled to the surface.

The shadow wrapped itself around me, blacking out the world.

PART II

Chapter 15

TWO MONTHS

I celebrated my two-month anniversary in the camp with a hot breakfast cooked outside the front of the lodge— fried rabbit and the last of the beans, cooked on the camping stoves. I'd tried the generator, which had worked, but it was also extremely noisy. I didn't need the attention it might bring.

The rabbit was delicious, if a little small. It was the first real protein I'd had for weeks. I don't count the jerky or the protein bars. I let out a little moan of pleasure as I sank my teeth into the succulent meat. I smiled, realizing how much like one of my zombie friends I must sound.

The flame on one of the stoves sputtered. I turned them both off—I was running low on gas. It was a sign that my situation was becoming more tenuous by the day—one of many.

I'd settled into a nice rhythm, spending my days reading or performing little maintenance tasks around the camp. Or hunting zombies. It had been several weeks since I'd seen a helicopter, and apart from the occasional zombie that wandered conveniently through the camp, no one had happened upon my little sanctuary.

A cloud passed overhead, and I shivered. The days were getting cooler as the summer drew to a close. I'd been lucky. The weather had been warm and dry, but winter would be here before I knew it. I had shelter, but when the temperatures dropped, I'd need heat, and that meant either lighting the fire in the lodge or running the generator. Neither of those options appealed to me, but before I had to make that choice, I needed to get some food. There were still some cardboard-flavored protein bars and a couple of cans of soup but not much else.

As I finished the meal, my confidence ebbed away. The shadow reprimanded me for ignoring the long-term practicalities of living in the camp. I needed to act, or I'd have to resort to eating the flesh of my subjects.

I dug out the hand-drawn map I'd found and laid it out on the ground. If it was right, Sally's Home Comforts was about six miles away, most of that on the highway.

I figured a couple of hours to get there, an hour or so looking for supplies. Depending on how much stuff I brought with me, it would take two or three more hours to get back. I knew it was a long shot—the chance of a stash of supplies lasting this long without being raided was virtually nil, but it was the only option I had.

Six hours away from the camp. The idea made me nervous. I'd be out in the open for much of the journey, exposed and vulnerable. Who knew what I'd find when I got there? There was still food in the lodge. I could wait a couple more days. Maybe I should find another subject before I left. I thought of my snare hanging in the workshop, and the shadow stirred.

I call it a snare in the absence of a better name, but it

was much more than that. Since my first successful capture, I'd made some improvements to my zombie-wrangling weapon of choice.

I'd found a thicker, stronger pole to use as the handle. I'd refined the noose itself to be more secure and easier to maneuver and tighten. And I'd added three blades taken from a couple of pairs of shears I'd found in the workshop. Two stuck out either side of the noose. They were short but enough to inflict some serious damage if required. The third blade was bigger and heavier and was attached to the opposite end of the pole. It had taken a while to get it properly secured, but with some creative metalwork I'd managed to bolt it into place. The snare was an effective tool. It was ideal for my purpose.

I took a deep breath and promised the shadow that I'd let it out to play again, *after* we had our supplies. I walked around the camp's perimeter before I left. That was a legitimate job, not procrastination. As always, I'd checked it as soon as I'd woken up, but that was just to make sure nothing had stumbled into the camp while I was sleeping. I still needed to perform my daily maintenance.

The perimeter was a mismatched collection of wire, string, rope, and fishing line that I'd hung with cans and strips of metal to act as an early warning system. The lines were at about chest height. It meant humans could easily crawl under them—because experience had taught me that putting the wire at ankle height meant getting woken up by every skunk, rabbit, and raccoon that came wandering through. Once I'd adjusted the height of the trip wires, my nights had been largely undisturbed. The only exception being three deer that turned up a couple of weeks earlier. If I'd kept the rifle nearer at hand, I might have been eating venison for weeks.

Satisfied the perimeter was still intact, and unable to think of any more reasons to delay, I grabbed my backpack, checked I had enough food and water, and set off toward Sally's Home Comforts.

I knew the first part of the route well—out the main camp entrance, along the trail to the logging road that would lead me to the highway. I kept to the grass verge, under the shelter of the trees. The sun wasn't as strong these days, and walking down the middle of the road would have made the journey easier, but I wanted to limit how much time I spent in the open.

About a mile later, I stopped to take a drink of water and check the map. If its creators were right, a few minutes down the road, a shortcut through the forest would take me directly to the highway. It was labeled Salvation Alley.

I'd used the map a couple of times in the past, and it was surprisingly accurate. Sure enough, ten minutes later, I found a handwritten sign nailed to a tree declaring the nearby path to be Salvation Alley. From here, the journey would be pretty straightforward—follow the trail for half a mile to the highway then three or four miles south to Sally's Home Comforts. Easy.

The trail was rough and uneven. Although the forest hadn't grown over it completely, it was littered with debris left there by winter storms and the natural decay of the forest. The obstacles slowed me down, but they may have also saved my life.

I was in sight of the highway when I heard a low droning sound. I crouched down and searched the sky for the noise's origin then realized it was coming from the road. A few moments later, four zombies wandered into view. Their feet dragged across the road's surface, scuffing out an irregular rhythm to accompany their monotone voices. Three more zombies appeared right behind them, and within minutes the road was a river of the living dead.

There were dozens of them. Men, women, children. Old, young. Black, white, Asian. Some were relatively intact; others sported serious damage—missing limbs or gaping gunshot wounds. The stench of death and decay wafted through the trees, and the droning sound just kept swelling along with their numbers.

If I hadn't been slowed down by the rough terrain, I'd have walked straight into them. Images of being caught on the road streamed through my head. I'd seen swarms a couple of times before—from the relative safety of a building. I'd also seen what happens to people caught in their path. It doesn't take long for a group of zombies to overwhelm their victims. One moment they're running for their lives, a few short seconds later, they disappear beneath the tearing, biting dead.

This swarm was at least three times the size of any I'd seen before. I wanted to run or at least retreat farther down the trail, but I was afraid of attracting their attention. One or two zombies I can handle. Well over a hundred? No.

Something cracked off to my right, and I turned to see a group of zombies pushing through the forest toward me. The swarm's growth had forced some of them off the road. They moved slowly, hampered by the undergrowth. None of them had seen me yet, but I didn't have much time before they did. I backed down the trail and then froze as another zombie stepped out of the trees and onto the path ahead of me. He cut directly across the trail, stumbling on a downed tree in the process. Another zombie, a teenager by the look of it, followed right behind him.

I dropped as low to the ground as possible, scanning the area around me for cover. The closest thing I could see to safety was a fir tree with a couple of branches low enough for me to climb up. I hesitated, trying to work out whether climbing the tree would be choosing the frying pan or the fire.

The zombies were still coming—three of them close by with at least ten more scattered through the forest behind them. The road was crowded with stumbling, groaning living dead. I went for the tree.

Chapter 16

A VIEW FROM ABOVE

I put the tree trunk between me and the zombies in the forest. The lowest branch was still a foot or so above my outstretched arms. I jumped, caught the branch, and hung there, legs swinging for a couple of seconds before my hands slipped. I dropped back to the ground. Picking a point nearer the trunk, I tried again. As soon as I was hanging from the branch, I started pulling myself up.

My feet fought for purchase on the trunk. After several heart-stopping seconds, I managed to roll myself onto the branch. The climb quickly became easier from there. I clambered up a couple more levels, high enough that I was well out of reach but not so far away that I couldn't see what was happening or tell if I'd been spotted. Not that I knew what I'd do if I had been.

I sat on the branch as the stench of the dead grew stronger. Another zombie stepped onto the trail—a woman with a deep split in the side of her head. Most of her clothes had been torn away to reveal the rotting, blue-gray flesh beneath. She moved painfully slowly across the path without looking up. As she passed beneath me, two more zombies stumbled into view. These were younger, fresher, and they moved more quickly than the woman. One of them stumbled into the tree I was in. He let out a low-pitched moan and moved away.

The third zombie slowed then stopped. He was right beneath me and so close, the smell was almost overpowering. Part of his leg had been torn away, leaving the muscle beneath exposed. Rot had set in, and the wound was a festering mass of decay. The creature let out a low moan and rocked left and right. The smell caught in my throat, and I started to gag. The reflex was so strong, I had to place my hand over my mouth. Every breath I took just made it worse.

The zombie turned his head toward the road and moaned again. He took an uneven step forward, away from the tree. I held my breath, closed my eyes. Every ounce of my concentration was focused on not throwing up. I held on as long as I could. My lungs burned.

Finally, I let out the breath and opened my eyes. The zombie was moving along the path to rejoin the rest of the swarm. The smell lingered, but it was less intense, bearable. I took shallow breaths and watched as the zombies filed past beneath me.

The swarm was huge. It took over half an hour for the bulk of it to pass by. Even then, there were still a handful of stragglers trailing behind—the zombies with more extreme injuries. I sat in the tree, watching them crawl past, until I was as sure as I could be that it was safe. Then I dropped down to ground level and made my way out to the road.

The highway was wide and straight, and I could still see the swarm's tail end off to my right. They were far enough away that I doubted they'd see me, but I was glad I was heading in the other direction.

I moved under cover of the trees and had a drink of

water, trying to wash the taste of decay from my mouth. A subtle rottenness still hung in the air. Here and there, scraps of clothing and spatters of dark fluid marked the swarm's passing. The water helped a little, but there was no shaking the remnants of terror still clinging to my mind. I had to get moving.

Taking one last look at the swarm, I tightened my backpack and turned south.

Chapter 17

REMAINS

Sally's Home Comforts was located at the bottom of a shallow valley and turned out to be a gas station and a combined restaurant and general store. Apart from a few broken windows, the restaurant and store were relatively intact, but someone had driven a semi into the gas station. The resultant fire had burned itself out but not before it had gutted the building. The concrete around the station was scorched, the heat so intense it had melted the canopy above the pumps into a twisted lump of blackened metal. The husk of the truck's cab was wedged inside the station itself.

I walked slowly across the road to the wreckage of the gas station. The concrete apron around the pumps was buckled and broken as though the tanks beneath had exploded. A ragged sheet of metal about ten feet long had torn through the ground. It looked like the fin of some sort of mechanical shark cutting through the earth. The truck was a twisted, charred mess. I smelled burned metal and rubber.

The building's supports had given way when the truck

had slammed through the front wall, and the concrete roof had collapsed. The top of the cab was folded into a V-shape. The windshield had shattered, and the resultant fragments crunched under my feet as I examined the interior of the building. The inferno had destroyed anything that might have been of use. The general store would be a better bet.

Metal creaked. There was movement inside the cab, and then a zombie's face appeared in the space between the crushed roof and the front of the truck. He let out a low, paper-thin groan. The thing's skin had been burned to a thick black crust. The opening was far too small for him to get through, but that didn't stop him from trying. He pressed his head into the gap. The roof's sharp edges dug into his cheeks, and a chunk flaked away. He made a high-pitched keening sound as though in pain. The cab doors were buckled, and there was no way for him to get out or for me to get in. Ignoring the shadow's disappointment, I moved on.

The fire had left black stains along the store's walls, but somehow most of the building had remained standing. The windows were also intact, but they were smeared with thick smudges of dry, black blood.

I circled the entire building. There was a large parking area out back. It was littered with chunks of rock and discarded car parts that I didn't recognize. A few meager patches of grass had managed to take hold, but otherwise, it was just a broad expanse of gray concrete.

A couple of abandoned cars stood near the building. One of them was empty, but I could see someone moving inside the other. The shadow urged me to investigate, but I ignored it and continued around to the front of the store.

There had been zombies there at some point. I could see signs of their passing—a hat, a couple of mismatched shoes. There were marks on the concrete, scattered patches of blood mostly, but no bodies. If there'd been anyone inside the building trying to survive, they hadn't taken down any of the zombies.

The front door was undamaged, but there was more blood, mostly smeared across the glass. I almost kicked it open without thinking, but I stopped myself. I pushed the door, and it opened. Surprised, I stepped into the small hallway that lay beyond. The air was dry and musty, with the familiar stench of death underlying the more mundane odors. I waited in the gloom, letting my eyes adjust.

A door lay ahead of me—plain, blue, and closed. A STAFF ONLY sign sat at about head height. It was slightly crooked. The restaurant was on my right. It was the type of roadside diner I'd seen in movies and on TV a dozen times but never actually been inside.

The general store was on my left, and the name was overstating its scale. It was small enough that having more than seven or eight customers at one time would upset a fire marshal. Three narrow aisles ran the length of the room. A small counter with a till on it sat next to the door. I didn't care about the size of the store. What I cared about was that the shelves that lined the aisles were still virtually untouched.

Half of them were filled with pointless knickknacks— mementos aimed at the stream of tourists that rolled through the mountains during the summer. But the rest held an array of food items chosen for their durability and convenience. There were cans of soup and chili, boxes of protein and energy bars, packets of noodles, and bags of the ever-present jerky. Combined, it was more than enough to last me through the winter and beyond. I just needed to get it back to the camp. There was even a pile of small propane bottles that would fit my stoves.

On foot, it would take me ten or more trips to get everything transported to the camp. And that was assuming I didn't run into a swarm. I could leave the camp and move into Sally's, but it was far more exposed. There was no way to set up the kind of perimeter I'd grown used to. More importantly, I'd need to find a new place for the shadow to work. So, moving wasn't an option, but I couldn't just ignore the supplies. I'd need to find some way to cut down the number of trips. I thought of the quad bikes. I could probably ride one, and there was plenty of room to carry supplies on the back. Even having to stick to the roads instead of using Salvation Alley, it would make things a lot quicker.

I walked out of the store and crossed the hallway into the restaurant. It, too, was mostly undisturbed. There were six tables and four booths. All of them were neatly laid out with knives, spoons, forks, napkins, menus, and condiments. The menu was small and basic, but the descriptions of the Early Riser Breakfast and Classic Blueberry Pancakes left my mouth watering and my stomach rumbling. I chewed on an energy bar as I walked around the rest of the room, but my stomach wasn't fooled.

A narrow service counter ran along the left-hand side of the room, with four stools lined up in front of it. Another worktop held a small coffee maker and space for the person working the counter to prepare some food. A doorway led into the kitchen, and when I saw it, I realized why the menu was so limited. It was tiny. There was barely enough space for one person to work in, and the fridge, stove, and microwave oven were equally compact.

There were more supplies in the kitchen, mostly the raw materials for making the specials. When I opened the fridge, I was greeted by a wave of rancid air filled with the stench of rotting meat and vegetables. I thought I saw a tub of blueberries just before I gagged and quickly swung the door shut.

The possibilities of the restaurant exhausted, I headed back out to the hallway and the STAFF ONLY door.

I'd grown used to the reek of death that permeated the building, but as I opened the door the stench grew stronger. The source of the smell was hanging from the center of the room—two corpses, a man and woman in their sixties. They'd fastened electrical cord around a metal beam running across the ceiling, climbed on top of two chairs from the restaurant, and put nooses around their necks before kicking the chairs away.

The window on the opposite side of the room told the rest of the story. There were no zombies pressed against it now, but the glass was covered with smears of blood and cracked in places where something had tried to get in.

The room was simply decorated with a three-seater couch that had seen better days, a low glass coffee table, and a couple of bookcases that held four books and a scattering of trinkets from around the world. There was a television in one corner that had probably been state of the art thirty years ago. Part of me doubted it would have been able to receive broadcasts, even without the disruption of the zombie apocalypse. Three more doors led out of the room; one of them was the exit to the parking area at the rear of the building.

I walked into the room, and the bodies stirred. The woman raised her head, revealing black eyes and a purple, bloated face. A cluster of flies rose up out of her blue-rinsed hair. She let out a low moan. The sound caught the atten-tion of the man hanging beside her. He, too, raised his equally bloated head. He reached out toward me, legs kicking. His movements started him swinging. He bumped against the woman, eliciting more throaty growls from the woman. I backed away from the twitching zombies a little. The electrical cords creaked as they moved but held firm.

The hairs on the back of my hands rose, the shadow making its presence felt. I looked around the room again, really taking in the table, the couch, the bookshelves. It had potential. I could see the possibilities.

I shook my head. I had my workshop. My sanctuary.

I moved around the room, staying out of reach of the zombies. They moaned and twisted as I passed near them.

One of the doors led to a tiny bathroom with a toilet and a shower. The walls were hand-painted with flowers, and a row of poppies ran along the bottom of the shower curtain. A desiccated block of solid air freshener hung from the ceiling, lending the room a faint smell of flowers.

The second interior door opened up onto a bedroom that was just big enough for a double bed. It was covered with a floral bedspread, and despite the decaying corpses next door, the air smelled of lavender.

I heard a soft thud and went back out to the living room. One of the man's slippers had fallen off, revealing a threadbare sock. His foot twitched as he strained to get at me. The cord around his neck was cutting into the flesh. His mouth dropped open, revealing a purple tongue. He groaned. It was a thick, wet sound, repulsive.

I walked past the struggling zombies to the bookcase and scanned the shelves. They contained a three-volume *Modern History of North America* and a Bible. The history books were heavy, but I put them in my pack anyway. I'd need something to get me through the winter. I left the Bible behind. If there is a God, he gave up on me a long time ago.

The woman moaned, and a dribble of black fluid seeped

over the edges of the cord around her neck. I knew I should kill them. If I was going to come back to the store for supplies, I needed to make sure it was safe. Leaving two zombies in the building was a stupid idea.

The shadow agreed, in its own way. I was safe here, it whispered. I could take advantage of my good fortune and set it free, right here, right now. Together, we could purge these two of their guilt.

Temptation gnawed at me. I even started to drag the coffee table over so that I could cut the man down. Then I stopped. Looking back, I don't know why. It just didn't seem right. The workshop was the shadow's domain—this was just an old couple's living room. I straightened the table and walked out of the room, making sure to close the door firmly behind me.

I went inside the store and grabbed as much propane, soup, chili, and energy bars as I could comfortably carry and put them into my backpack. I hesitated when I reached the packets of jerky but ended up taking four and sliding them into the pack's front pocket—I might have hit the mother lode, but I couldn't get complacent. There were some generic painkillers behind the counter, and I took those, too.

The pack rattled as I settled it on my back. I adjusted the straps so that it didn't slip as I walked. It was heavy. Thankfully, I didn't have a lot of hills to climb on the way back.

Outside, the wind had picked up, bringing a few clouds with it. I was glad for the break from the sun, but they held the threat of rain. A heavy thunderstorm could make the trails almost impassable. I checked the front door was closed then set off home.

By the time I got back to Camp Redfern, I was hungry, the cans of soup were digging into my spine, and I was beginning to regret picking up the books. The end result of all those distractions was that I was halfway across the camp by the time I noticed the door to the lodge was open. I cursed and ran, half crouched, to Cabin Two. I pressed myself up against the side of the building and removed my knife.

The backpack was slowing me down, but I didn't have time to remove it before an ungainly young man with dark hair hanging to his shoulders came out of the lodge. His face was thin and as awkward as the rest of him. A straggly beard clung to his neck and chin. His hands were raised above his head. I tensed when I saw him, my grip tightening on the knife. I regretted not taking the rifle with me when I left the camp.

"It's okay; we're not here to cause trouble!"

He was shouting, and the sound made me wince. If there were any zombies nearby, he'd bring them right down on top of us, although maybe that would be for the best.

The man had obviously seen me; he was looking toward Cabin Two and my hiding place. He moved to the edge of the walkway and called again. "Please! We just need some help. Our friend is hurt."

Our friend. That meant at least three people, possibly more. The world tilted a little and threatened to throw me onto the ground. I leaned against the cabin, focusing on the pack's metal frame digging into my back until everything righted itself again. When I risked another look, the man was still standing there, hands still raised.

I could run, hide, go back to sleeping in trees. I had food and the river for water. There might be another camp to the north or maybe something even better. My tools were in the workshop, but I could go around the camp to get them. It seemed like the smartest option. I straightened up, ready to slip into the forest and be gone. And then the man called again.

"Please! We're so tired. We just need a place to sleep. Even for one night."

The shadow flickered to life. Already awakened by the discovery of the old couple, this latest development had it intrigued. Now there were other possibilities, other ways to gain satisfaction.

I walked out from behind the cabin.

As soon as he saw me, the young man started talking. "We're not here to cause any problems, I promise. Our friend is hurt." He must have seen something in my face because he held his hands out toward me and started talking even more quickly. "No, no, he wasn't bit. Nothing like that. He's got a fever or something. That's all. He's not a biter."

I stopped a few feet away from the lodge, the knife held out in front of me in what I hoped was a threatening manner.

"What's your name?" I'd managed to force some confidence into my voice, but it felt odd to be face-to-face with someone, having a conversation.

"I'm Alex. Lucy and Mike are inside."

"And that's all? There's only three of you?"

"Yeah, just three."

"Where did you come from?"

"Me and Mike are from Seattle. We met just outside the city. I got cornered by one of the biters, and he got me out of there. We met Lucy, and... We met Lucy a week later. She was hiding out in a house, but she'd run out of food."

It all seemed plausible enough. "Why come north? Why not stay in the city?"

"Biters, man. There's packs of them everywhere. And the people are even worse. The military is trying to build walls and create a safe zone, but there ain't nowhere safe anymore."

I thought back to the swarm I'd seen on the road. Hopefully, this trio hadn't led it to the camp. "How did you find this place?"

The young man pointed to his left. "The river. We were following it north and looking for somewhere Mike could rest when we found the camp. That's it, man. I promise."

A shadow moved across one of the lodge's windows. I tensed. "Bring the others out."

Alex called inside, and a few seconds later a woman in her midthirties appeared in the doorway.

"Come out!" I called.

The woman, Lucy presumably, stood next to Alex. She didn't raise her hands, but she watched the knife.

"Where's Mike?" I said.

"Inside sleeping," Lucy said. "He's hurt. He slipped down a slope and hit his head on a rock. He isn't infected."

"How long ago did it happen?"

"Two days, almost three." She took a step toward me. "Please, we need somewhere to rest. Just until Mike's fever breaks. We can help out here, keep watch for you and the others."

I didn't understand. "Others?"

Lucy frowned. "You mean... you're the only person living here?"

I cursed my stupidity even as I considered trying to lie.

"But what about the stuff in the cabins?" Alex said.

He'd been exploring. Did that mean they'd also found the path to the workshop, maybe even the workshop itself? I began to panic until I realized that if they had, they wouldn't be just standing there talking to me.

"You've been in the cabins?"

Alex had begun to lower his hands, but he held them out in front of him again. "No! No. I just looked through the window, just quickly. We needed to know if there was anyone here. I didn't go in, just in case. Those biters get everywhere."

I rubbed my hand across my chin as I tried to think of a way out of this. I might be holding the knife, but I was the one at a disadvantage.

I waved the weapon toward them. "Where else have you been?"

Alex pointed his thumb over his shoulder. "Just the crapper, man, I swear."

I raised my eyebrows at the woman, and she nodded. Again, I considered leaving—abandoning the camp to these interlopers and retreating to the forest. Maybe I could move to Sally's Home Comforts after all. If I took the map with me, they might never find it. But someone else would. Eventually.

I lowered the knife. "Show me your friend."

Chapter 18
INTRUDERS

Lucy and Alex led me inside to the couch where Mike was lying. He was Asian—Chinese or Japanese maybe—and wearing dark blue jeans and a paler blue shirt. He was unconscious, his face beaded with sweat. He had a grimy bandage stuck to his forehead. It was stained with blood and starting to come loose. A damp cloth lay on the coffee table next to the couch. Blood had dripped across his left shoulder, staining the shirt, but it looked like it had come from his head wound.

He murmured softly as I approached, but it was the sound of someone dreaming, not the mindless droning of a zombie. I checked around his body, searching for bites without touching him. As far as I could tell he was clean. I looked at Lucy. She held my gaze, determined, ready to respond if I tried to force them to leave.

"You can stay one day," I said.

It seemed like a fair compromise, but Lucy shook her head. "Please, we need a few days. Until Mike has recovered. Then we'll leave."

"Please, man," Alex said. He ran his fingers through his hair, tugging at it. The knuckles on his right hand were grazed.

I was ready to tell them no, that they had to leave, but the shadow cut off the words.

Instead, I nodded. "Okay, just until he's better."

"Thank you," Lucy said. "We're very grateful, and we'll leave as soon as Mike's well enough to travel."

Alex grinned. "Thanks, man. You've saved our lives. Literally."

"I should have some antibiotics. I'll get them." I didn't really want to give the tablets away, but if it would help get them out of the camp, it was worth it.

They both thanked me.

I walked toward the dining room.

Lucy called after me. "What's your name?"

I hesitated and considered telling the truth. Then I said, "Marcus Black."

Lucy smiled and nodded. "Thank you, Marcus."

I shrugged, hopeful it would imply it wasn't a big deal, and went to the kitchen.

I swung my backpack up onto the table and removed the supplies I'd scavenged from the store. The only drugs I'd picked up were the painkillers. I picked up one of the containers and then retrieved the antibiotics from the cupboard above the sink. There were less than a dozen tablets left. The sight of them lying in the bottom of the container made me clench my teeth.

The shadow whispered to me, reminding me that there was an easy solution to the problem. My hand moved to the knife on my belt before I could stop it. I pictured myself cutting Lucy's throat while she tended to Mike. Alex would be harder to surprise. He'd see me killing her, and he was taller than me and probably heavier. I shook my head. No, I didn't need to kill them.

I considered holding some of the antibiotics back. I'd been lucky so far, but it was inevitable I'd get an infection at some point. Especially working so closely with the dead. In the end, I left all the tablets in the bottle. I put my backpack in the corner of the room and took the antibiotics and painkillers through to Lucy, along with a glass of water.

She thanked me and managed to get one of the tablets down Mike's throat.

"Will that help?" Alex said.

"There's not enough for a full course," Lucy said, "but I hope so."

The shadow eased back into my mind. I'd need to act before Mike recovered. I dismissed the thought. He'd get better, and then they'd leave.

Lucy, Alex, and I spent the day circling each other, warily—exchanging brief snippets of small talk when we had to but for the most part keeping busy and out of each other's way.

As night fell, they gained a haunted, nervous look and glanced nervously toward the window so often I don't think they even knew they were doing it. If I'd doubted that they'd spent time sleeping rough in the forest, that look would have eased those fears. I recognized it from my own face—too much time waiting for death to come stumbling out of the shadows.

They took turns watching Mike. Even though I'd gone through my normal checks and the perimeter would warn us if any zombies happened our way, they insisted on acting as lookouts for the camp itself as well.

When I went upstairs to my room, I left Lucy sitting by the window, watching for signs of danger while Alex snored loudly in the armchair. She was tense, nervous. The relative safety of the lodge seemed to have done nothing to dull the memories of whatever horrors she'd seen.

After my trip to the store, I was tired. My arms and legs were aching, and there were two red marks on my shoulders from the backpack.

Despite my weariness, I couldn't sleep. I lay in bed, thinking about the other people in the lodge. Their presence stuck in my mind like grains of sand—grist for my thoughts. No matter how I tried to distract myself, no matter what tricks I played, my brain kept dragging me back to the existence of strangers in my sanctuary.

I felt violated.

The shadow was restless. It muttered in my ear. It insisted that these new arrivals were an opportunity not a threat. The shadow could sense their guilt. It was draped around them like a cloak and oozed from the pores in their skin.

The zombies we'd killed had provided a release for the shadow, but these people ignited memories of the years before the outbreak. The lodge was a perfect location to resume my true calling.

I resisted. I'd always picked solitary targets; it was safer that way. Even with Mike injured, it was too risky. I'd survived this long by being careful. This wasn't the time to throw that caution away.

I lay in bed, battling with the shadow, for what felt like hours. Eventually, exhaustion won out, but my dreams were filled with imagined confrontations with Lucy and Alex. All of them culminated in the same thing—the discovery of the workshop and my handiwork and the two of them turning on me.

Chapter 19

THE CULT

I woke early, hoping to get some time to make sure I hadn't left any incriminating evidence lying around the lodge, but the intruders were already up. Lucy was tending to Mike while Alex made breakfast. She'd removed the old bandage and was dabbing Mike's brow with a wet cloth. The cut on his head was deep and crusted with blood, the edges an angry red.

The smell of food hit me as soon as I opened the kitchen door. Alex had found the supplies I'd brought back from the store and was cooking vegetable soup on one of the portable gas stoves. The smell made my mouth water.

He heard me enter the kitchen and gestured toward the table. "Morning. Grab a bowl."

My immediate reaction was anger. This was my home. These people had come here uninvited. I'd let them stay but only under duress. Now they were treating the lodge as though it was a hotel. At least he hadn't tried to get the generator working.

Lucy walked into the kitchen. "How's breakfast coming along?"

"I'm not sure soup is really breakfast, but it's ready when you are."

Lucy smiled and grabbed a bowl.

She gestured to me to go first, but I shook my head. "No, go on."

"Thanks."

I watched her spoon the soup into her bowl. She looked worn down, but there was determination in her eyes. I wasn't sure how Alex had managed to live through the early days of the outbreak, but Lucy's strength was obvious. I'd need to be careful around her.

"What's that?" Alex said.

He walked out of the kitchen and through the back door. Frowning, Lucy followed him. I hesitated for a moment and then did the same.

Outside, Alex was staring up into the sky. His brow was furrowed in concentration.

Panic hit me as I realized the sound he'd heard was an incoming helicopter.

"Get inside!" I said.

I urged them back into the lodge. Alex followed my instructions, but Lucy stood her ground. I put my hand on her shoulder, trying to get her to move.

She batted it away. "They can pick us up!"

"No!" I said.

"Why not?"

The sound of the helicopter grew louder. "Come on, it's not safe."

Lucy half turned to go inside, but she was still reluctant. "What do you mean, not safe?"

I beckoned to her, desperately searching for an excuse. "There's no time to explain. Come on!"

Finally, she gave in and followed Alex into the lodge.

Once they were both inside, I checked the sky. There was no sign of the chopper, but the sound of its engine was getting louder by the second. I ducked inside, swung the door shut, and bolted it.

I went to the window, searching for the helicopter and running over everything that had happened since the others had arrived.

Was there anything outside that would show the camp was inhabited? I was always careful not to leave any signs of life out in the open. My perimeter alarm was a calculated risk. The wires and cans were too small to be spotted from the air. But I couldn't be sure Alex and Lucy hadn't changed something.

What about heat signatures? If the army was using some sort of infrared camera to look for survivors, they might see the heat from the lodge. Visions of the military touching down in the clearing behind the building flashed through my head. I slammed my hand against the wall in frustration.

Lucy appeared at my side. "What the hell is going on?"

I raised my hand to cut her off as the helicopter roared over the building. There was no gunner this time, and its side door was closed. I hoped that was a good thing.

"Marcus," Lucy said. "Tell us why we aren't outside, trying to flag down that helicopter."

I waited until the aircraft was out of sight then turned to her. "It's not safe."

Her lips pursed slightly before she spoke. "You said that. *Why* isn't it safe?"

I grasped at the excuses flickering through my head, clinging to the first one that sounded plausible. "They aren't the military."

Lucy frowned. "Then who are they?"

"They're some sort of gang. A cult maybe." She looked

skeptical, but I carried on, the lies slipping neatly into place. "I ran into them in the forest a couple of weeks ago and only just got away. If they find us here, they'll kill us, if we're lucky."

"And this cult has a helicopter?"

"Yes, they must have found it somewhere. There's junk like that all over the place."

Lucy moved past me and looked out the window. "If it was them, they've gone now."

"It's for the best, believe me. I saw what they do to people."

Alex winced. "Sounds like we had a lucky escape."

When Lucy didn't respond, he put a hand on her shoulder. "Come on, Luce, let's get something to eat."

She nodded, still staring after the helicopter. Eventually, the two of them went back into the kitchen, leaving me in the dining room with my stomach twisted into knots.

Chapter 20
PERIMETER

I ate my breakfast of lukewarm vegetable soup in the kitchen while Lucy tended to Mike. Alex sat in the dining room. He seemed to have been taken in by my story —a post-apocalyptic cult probably fit very well with his pop culture–inspired expectations.

Lucy hadn't bought it. She didn't challenge me, but she barely said a word as Alex dished out the food. I'd considered following her into the lounge to try to make conversation, but I didn't want to have to embellish my story further. Lies are best kept short and to the point.

Once I'd finished the soup, I went out onto the bench behind the lodge. There were a few clouds in the sky, but otherwise, it was another idyllic day. It was as though nature were trying to compensate for the horrors mankind had unleashed by stringing together endless weeks of good weather.

The lodge door opened, and Alex came out. He stood near the bench, gazing out across the clearing as though he was searching for something. I let him stand there, happy with the silence, but after a couple of minutes he turned his attention to me. "Is there really a gang out there? With a helicopter?"

I shifted on the bench. "Yes, there is."

"And their camp's close by?"

"I think so."

"Is that how come they nearly caught you? They found this place?"

"No, that was before I came here."

Alex ran his hand through his hair, pulling it into a ponytail before letting go again. "So... what happened?"

I took a deep breath then let it out again. I put on a pained expression as though I were dredging up memories I'd prefer stayed buried. "I'd rather not talk about it."

"I shouldn't have asked. Sorry."

I waved his apology away.

Alex looked out toward the forest. His eyes grew distant, and he rubbed at his arm, as though he was cold. "There's some dark spirits out there, man. Really dark."

He might not have been the smartest person I'd ever met, but he was right about that, and they were closer than he thought. "That sounds like you're speaking from experience?"

Alex nodded slowly, but before he could elaborate the back door opened, and Lucy stepped out into the sunshine. She exchanged a look I couldn't read with Alex, and he stayed quiet.

"There's bloodstains upstairs in one of the bedrooms," she said. "Do you know how they got there?"

I thought I could detect a hint of accusation in her voice. She'd been snooping around. Maybe she'd even gone into my room. Did she think I'd killed someone?

"It was the counselors from the camp."

"The ones from the photo on the stairs?"

"Yes, they killed themselves."

Alex sucked in a breath and muttered something I couldn't hear.

"Where are the bodies?" Lucy said.

I gestured over my shoulder. "I buried them in the forest, away from the camp."

"What about the others?"

I frowned as though I didn't know what she meant.

"From the cabins. There's cases and clothes in a couple of them."

I caught myself about to look in the direction of the workshop and stopped, hoping she hadn't noticed. "I don't know. There's no sign of them. Other than the clothes, I mean."

"Maybe they went for help?" Alex said.

I shrugged but didn't speak.

"Maybe," Lucy said.

I avoided her gaze while still trying not to look guilty. The inquisition was making me tense, but the shadow was reveling in the attention.

There was a pause, just long enough to become awkward, then Alex said, "I'm going to take a look around."

"Be careful," Lucy said.

"Don't worry, I'll stay close."

I tried to think of some way of discouraging him, but my mind went blank. He wandered out onto the grass, toward the forest and the path to the workshop.

Lucy came over to the bench and sat down. I shifted sideways to give her some more room then instantly wondered whether that made me seem more or less guilty.

"How is he?" I said. "Your friend, I mean."

"Mike? He's okay. Still unconscious, but I think the antibiotics are helping. Thanks for letting us have them."

I thought of how small the bottle of pills was and how likely it was that I'd need antibiotics myself at some point. "It's not a big deal."

"Well, thank you anyway." Lucy's voice was soft, all trace of suspicion gone for now. Did that mean I was in the clear, or was she just setting a trap for me to stumble into?

Something cracked in the forest to our right, and we both turned to look. Alex was at the opposite end of the clearing and didn't notice. The noise came again, and then a pair of crows took off into the sky, squawking as they chased each other. Lucy's shoulders relaxed, but she kept her eyes fixed on the trees.

"It changes people," she said, quietly. "Having to fight for survival, constantly worrying about dying."

"No, it doesn't change people. It reveals who they really are."

Lucy looked at me. There was sadness in her eyes, deep and painful. "Do you really think that?"

I pretended to consider the question for a moment. "Yes. I do."

Lucy shook her head. "I can't believe that's true. I won't."

She looked at me, her eyes boring into mine. I think she was daring me to disagree with her. When I didn't respond, she turned back to the forest. Her gaze wandered around the edge of the clearing. She was looking for something, or someone.

When she spoke again, the sadness had gone from her voice, replaced by her normal confident self. "Do you have a map of this area?"

Fear trickled down my spine. The map was in my backpack in the kitchen. It was only a matter of time before someone found it, and then they'd know the helicopter was probably from the ranger station, not some psychopathic gang.

"No," I said, "but I wish I did."

"Where did the supplies come from?"

"There's a store a few miles southwest. It hasn't been raided, so there's lots of food there."

"Is it safe?"

"No. I walked right into the middle of a swarm on the way there."

"A swarm?"

"That's what I call a big group of zombies."

Lucy nodded. "We've met a couple, twenty or thirty zombies in each."

I gave a little laugh. "There were well over a hundred in the group I met. I had to hide in a tree."

Lucy's eyebrows flicked upward, her eyes wide. Her lips curved into a slight smile. "A tree? That must have been interesting."

"If by interesting you mean a terrifying experience I'd rather not repeat, then yes."

"How did you find the store? If you don't have a map."

"I passed it on the way here. I'm pretty good at remembering where things are."

"Boy Scout?"

I laughed again and shook my head.

Alex had made it to the far side of the clearing, and he was getting closer to the path that led to the workshop. He hadn't seen it yet. I'd been careful not to disturb the bushes disguising the gap in the trees, but I still grew tenser with every step he took toward it.

"Are you okay?" Lucy said.

I frowned. "Yes. I was just thinking... about my trip to the store."

"Was that when you met the gang?" The hint of skepticism was back in her voice.

"No, that was after the store."

"I thought you said it was a couple of weeks ago?"

"Yes, it was. I meant after I found the store the first time. The second time I didn't see the gang. Just the swarm."

Alex was getting closer to the path, and that, combined with Lucy's questions, was making me uncomfortable.

"Ah okay," she said.

There was a cough from inside the lodge.

Lucy stood to go back inside. I kept watching Alex.

"Do you have any more blankets?" Lucy said. "I need to keep Mike warm."

Alex was a couple of feet away from the entrance to the pathway. "I think there's some upstairs. In the second room. I'm in the first one."

Lucy said something, but I was already moving across the grass toward Alex. He was peering through the trees, trying to pull the bushes aside to get onto the trail.

I called out to him. "Alex?"

He half turned toward me. "Yeah?"

"I need your help."

"Sure, anything."

I moved around Alex so that I was between him and the pathway. "We've got to check the perimeter. Make sure nothing brought it down in the night."

Alex nodded enthusiastically. "Okay, no problem. Just tell me what to do."

I put my hand on his shoulder and guided him away from the trail. "We'll start over there, on the east side."

Alex nodded, and we set off across the grass. Behind him, I could see Lucy standing outside the lodge, watching us. Watching me.

Alex and I walked around the camp, checking the perimeter wires were still intact. He talked constantly, vomiting out words without really saying anything. For my part, I stuck to grunts of acknowledgment and the occasional vague comment. That seemed to be enough for him. He was quite happy to prattle on with minimal interruption. One part of me wanted to ask questions, but another was tired of interacting with people and was content to let him talk.

We were about halfway around the camp, close to the path that led down to the river, when a quiet scuffling noise came from the nearby undergrowth. Alex froze, his jabbering cut short. A squirrel burst from beneath a nearby bush and darted in front of us. Its tail brushed one of the tin cans hanging from the perimeter, setting it clattering.

Alex clutched at his heart. "Whoa." He was laughing, but his voice was uneven, and his skin was pale. He let out a slow breath and rubbed his forehead. I watched him closely as he looked off into the forest, eyes flicking left and right, searching for something.

"It was only a squirrel," I said.

He half smiled. "Yeah."

I focused on checking the can the squirrel had disturbed while Alex recovered. As we moved on around the camp, he kept his eyes on the forest. He didn't talk, just rubbed at the graze on his knuckles and left me to make sure the perimeter was set up correctly.

"So, what happened?" I said, pointing to the graze.

"Huh?" He looked down at his hand as though he'd forgotten it was there. "Oh... I scraped it on a rock when I was out getting wood for a fire. No biggie."

"There's some antiseptic cream in the lodge; you should put some of that on it. No point risking an infection."

"Sure, good idea. Thanks." He nodded, but his attention was still somewhere else.

As we got closer to the lodge, I stopped to tighten a length of string that I'd wrapped around a young tree. Alex stood next to me, still watching the forest. He frowned and tilted his head.

"You see something?" I said.

"Yes... no... probably not. I think it's just a shadow."

I followed his gaze, but the forest looked empty. By the time I'd finished with the string, the frown had gone, but Alex was still watching.

I stepped in front of him. "What's wrong? You're looking for something."

He hesitated, just for a second. "No, it's nothing. Nothing's wrong."

I wouldn't have thought it was possible, but the guy was a worse liar than I was. Apparently, we all had secrets. I let it pass and moved on along the perimeter. He followed a few seconds behind me.

When we got back to the lounge, Mike was sitting up on the couch. Lucy had dragged over one of the armchairs to be next to him. She'd found a couple of blankets upstairs and had wrapped them around his shoulders. Dark rings curved beneath his eyes. His forehead was slick with sweat. I'd met zombies that looked more alive. As Alex and I walked into the room, Mike coughed. His chest made a harsh rattling sound.

Alex broke into a grin as soon as he saw Mike was awake. "Hey, you're finally back in the land of the living."

Mike nodded, but he was looking past Alex at me.

Lucy leaned in toward him. "This is the person I was telling you about. Marcus."

Mike smiled. "Hey, Marcus. Forgive me if I don't get up.

I'm still feeling pretty unsteady." He raised a hand to the cut on his head. "Thanks for letting us stay here; we really appreciate it. And for the antibiotics. I hear you probably saved my life."

"That's okay," I said, trying to sound like I meant it. "It's just until you're back on your feet."

"Definitely, we don't want to encroach on—" Another rattling, wheezing cough interrupted him. Lucy touched his back, her face creased in concern.

It took him a full thirty seconds to get his breathing under control. He wiped the back of his hand across his mouth. "Sorry about that."

I shook my head in response.

"What I was trying to say was that we don't want to encroach on your territory. We'll be out of your hair as soon as possible."

"Thank you," I said.

We stood, frozen in our respective positions, until Lucy spoke. "Everything okay out there, Alex?"

"Errr. Sure, yeah. Yeah, it's all good."

The room fell silent again.

Alex shifted his feet then said, "I thought I could check out the river, see if I can catch us some fish. Unless anyone needs me here?"

"That sounds like a good idea," Mike said. "Fresh sushi would make a change from that jerky."

Lucy laughed. "Yes, that would be good. Thanks."

"Any fishing gear around here?" asked Alex.

I shook my head. "Not as far as I know. I haven't seen any."

Alex stuck out his bottom lip and bobbed his head. "In that case, I guess I'll just have to grab them out of the water with my bare hands. Like a bear." He grimaced and made a swiping motion with clawed hands.

Lucy rolled her eyes. "Go on, get out of here. Get back before it even thinks about getting dark, okay?"

It was Alex's turn to roll his eyes. "Yes, Mom," he said, grinning.

"And..." Mike said.

All three of them spoke in unison. "Watch your backside."

They laughed, the phrase apparently a tradition born out of repetition and shared experience. There was an easiness to their manner. It was as though now that Mike was on the road to recovery they could relax.

I smiled along with their laughter, but my stomach was twisting into knots. I didn't want Alex wandering around the forest on his own.

"Do you need any help?" I said. "With the fish, I mean."

"No, no. I'm good. Thanks, though."

"It might be safer with two of us."

Alex wrinkled his nose. "Nah, it's fine. Mike, you take it easy. Luce, look after him, okay?"

Lucy smiled.

"You just get us some fish," Mike said.

Alex left the lodge. We could hear him whistling the dwarfs' song from *Snow White* as he walked across the camp toward the river. Through the window, I watched him go.

"I'm going to let you get some rest," I said, as soon as Alex was out of sight. "I have some traps out in the forest that I should check. Maybe there'll be some rabbit to go with the fish."

"That would be great," Mike said.

"Okay then, I'll be an hour or so. I'll watch my backside,"

I said, trying to smile. Mike returned the joke with a broad grin, but Lucy's mouth barely moved.

I headed into the kitchen, put a couple of energy bars in my pocket, and grabbed a bottle of water. When I got outside, I hesitated. Yesterday morning I'd been happy and relaxed. Now I was tense, nervous. My stomach was still twisted up, and my throat was dry. I could feel the muscles taut across my shoulders, and my back was tight. It was all because of these people. Especially Lucy. She didn't trust me, and it was upsetting the equilibrium I'd built over the last couple of months.

Why had I said I'd be gone for so long? I did have a couple of traps, but they wouldn't take long to check. I'd have to find somewhere to hide in the forest.

The shadow writhed inside me, talking to me and planting ideas. The workshop would solve that problem. I could escape, find a zombie, and restore my balance. No, it was too dangerous with the intruders here.

Plates clattered in the kitchen behind me. Lucy was standing in the window. I waved at her and set off across the grass, picking the corner farthest away from the path to the workshop.

As soon as I got out of sight of the lodge, I moved east, around the camp. It was tough going, making my way through the undergrowth. I had my knife, but it was too small to cut through the vines and bushes that clogged the ground. Twice I had to backtrack and pick a different route. I didn't really know where I was going until I reached the river.

There was no sign of Alex. He'd been lying; he was probably back at the camp with Lucy and Mike. They'd be going through my things, looking for evidence to confirm their suspicions. Ice-cold fear flooded my system. The world swam around me. I had to close my eyes and lean against a tree.

I counted to sixteen then took a deep breath and opened my eyes. I decided to check the river before I went back to the camp. Alex might be farther upstream. Or downstream. I picked my way along the tree line, staying a few feet inside the forest so that I was always in shadow.

I went upstream for no other reason than it was easier. It turned out to be the right choice. Alex was around a bend, about a hundred feet from the trail to the camp. At some point, he'd ducked completely under the water because his hair was wet and hung around his shoulders like seaweed. He'd found a spot where the water was slow and waded out until it was waist height. He was standing, bent over, hands plunged deep into the water.

Alex stood there, not moving for several minutes, then swept his hands together and scooped them out of the water. If he'd been trying to catch a fish, he'd failed. Then he stuck his arms into the river and went back to standing still.

He repeated the process four or five times. Each time he came up empty-handed. He didn't seem concerned about standing there in the open, and I wondered how he'd react if a zombie came out of the water at him. I'd seen zombies trying to cross rivers before. They'd been swept away by the current, ending up who knew where. Alex might grab at something passing between his hands, only to find it was the still living remains of a human being, not a fish. He'd react too slowly, and it would be on him, tearing out his throat before he had a chance to get away.

But there were more disturbing scenarios, too. What if the helicopter came back? Alex seemed to have bought my story, but I couldn't be sure he wouldn't try to flag them down. If the machine gun was manned, Alex might see they were wearing uniforms, and he'd know I was lying.

He plunged his hands into the river once more, but they came back out empty.

A voice whispered in my ear. He was exposed, vulnerable. Anything could happen to him out here. It was a perfect opportunity for me to take the first step toward reclaiming the camp as my own.

I pressed my hand against the hilt of my knife. The shadow rose up. The edges of the forest receded, seeming to draw away to give me room to approach Alex.

My knife was in my hand, and I'd taken a couple of steps toward the river before I realized and stopped myself. I closed my eyes and counted to four, listening to the river and willing it to wash away the shadow.

Beneath the rushing water, I could hear the pounding of a heart. Whether it was mine or Alex's, I couldn't tell. The knife was weightless in my hand. It felt right. That was where it belonged. I counted to four again, breathing deeply. This wasn't the time. Even if I could get to Alex, the shadow would leave me exposed. If Lucy or Mike came looking for him, they'd find me at my most vulnerable. Another breath, another count of four.

The shadow loosened its grip.

When I opened my eyes again, the knife felt heavier. It was awkward, like it was too big for my hand. I took four deliberate steps back, deeper into the forest, and slipped the knife into its sheath. A shudder ran up my spine, my hands were shaking, and my stomach churned uneasily—parting gifts from the shadow.

Alex leaned back, stretching his arms, and glanced over his shoulder. I froze, suddenly sure he'd be able to see me. But his eyes passed over my hiding place without registering my presence. He returned his arms to the river. I let out the breath I'd been holding.

It looked like Alex really was just trying to catch some fish. He hadn't been using it as a cover for checking out the workshop. Unless... I thought back to the morning's events. Had Alex spent time with Lucy and Mike? Had he told them about the path?

My heart stuttered, and a sick feeling washed through my stomach. He didn't need to have told her. She'd *seen* us. I'd stopped Alex going into the forest by distracting him with talk about the perimeter, and she'd been watching me. The fishing wasn't the distraction; Alex was.

I backed farther into the forest as quickly as I dared. As soon as I was out of earshot, I turned and ran toward the lodge.

Chapter 21

AN INTERROGATION

When I broke out of the forest, Lucy was standing on the lodge's walkway, her eyes on the tree line. I was panting, and I had a scratch on my cheek where a branch had caught me in the face. I slowed but not quickly enough to avoid her noticing me running.

Her eyes widened. "What's the matter? Did you see someone?" The words came quickly, and there was real fear in her voice.

I raised a hand and took a few deep breaths, trying to ease the stitch that was developing in my side.

"No, nothing's the matter."

Her frown deepened. "So, what's the hurry?"

I tried a smile. "Just trying to get some exercise."

Lucy nodded, but she was frowning. "Any luck?"

My mind went blank. "Luck?"

"With the traps? You were checking them."

I was an idiot. "Ah right. No. No luck today. To be honest, I haven't caught anything with them for a while."

Lucy looked over my shoulder. "In that case, it's a good thing Alex has brought us something to eat."

Alex walked across the camp, two large fish in his hands and a huge grin on his face. "Sushi, anyone?"

Lucy smiled as he walked past her into the lodge. "I'm impressed. Maybe you aren't such a dead weight after all."

Alex laughed. "Come on, all this manly hunter stuff has made me hungry."

Lucy followed him inside. I paused. She'd asked me whether I'd seen some*one*, not some*thing*. She was more afraid of the living than the dead. Puzzled, I went inside.

Mike had moved from the couch into one of the armchairs. He'd changed his clothes as well, into jeans and a T-shirt. I recognized them from the psychedelic cabin and felt a twinge of anger. The change had done him some good. He looked healthier and more alert than he had less than an hour earlier.

Alex and Lucy took the fish into the kitchen, leaving me standing just inside the door. I was trying to think of a reason to skip food and go upstairs to my room, but before I could make my excuses, Mike said, "Can we have a chat? I'd like to know more about the situation here."

I smiled a little then sat down in the chair opposite him.

"Any trouble out there?" he said.

"No, no sign of anyone."

If he picked up on my use of anyone, it didn't register on his face.

"Good. Luce tells me you ran into a gang?"

Damn. "Yes."

"And they have a chopper?" His eyebrows were raised, and I could feel the skepticism hanging in the air around us.

"Yeah, they must have found it somewhere."

"Military?"

I shrugged. "Maybe, but I didn't get a close look at it. I was too busy running for my life."

"That bad, huh?"

I nodded but said nothing, hoping to starve the conversation of oxygen.

He opened his mouth to speak, but a coughing fit cut him off.

"I should let you rest."

He pressed one hand against his mouth and raised the other. "No, please."

I waited until he'd gotten the cough under control.

"I'm sorry," he said. "I was starting to give you the third degree there. Old habits die hard."

"Habits?"

"I'm a cop. Or I was until the world went to hell."

I tensed. "Like an... actual cop?"

"Yeah, in Seattle."

All I could think of to say was, "That's interesting."

I hoped the fear that was bubbling up inside me hadn't reached my voice. There were a lot of people I didn't want to be nosing around my home, but suspicious policemen were close to the top of the list, right beneath human lie detectors. Something in the kitchen clattered to the floor, and I jumped. I glanced at Mike and felt another wave of anxiety building.

He laughed. "Don't worry, I'm not going to arrest you for killing zombies."

I forced a smile and tried to ignore the trickle of sweat running down my back. I was about to make another move toward my bedroom when Alex came into the lounge. He was carrying a broad serving plate and grinning again. The plate held a mound of fish that had been inexpertly hacked from the bone, and a few crackers. Lucy followed him into the room with a jug of water, four glasses, and some forks.

Alex placed the fish down on the table. "Sorry there's no wasabi, guys."

I looked at the mass of gray-white flesh on the plate, and my stomach lurched. I stood, the sudden movement making me sway slightly as the blood rushed to my head. The room shifted around me. I squeezed my eyes shut, playing up my discomfort. When I opened them again, everyone was looking at me.

"I should go upstairs and get some rest," I said. "I'm not feeling very well."

"Are you sure?" Lucy said.

I nodded, and the room shifted on its axis again. "Yeah, I just didn't sleep well last night."

"At least take some food up with you," Alex said. "I'll get you a plate."

He turned to go out to the kitchen, but I put my hand on his shoulder. "No, please. It's fine. I'm not that keen on sushi anyway."

"Totally get it. No worries. You could take some crackers."

"No, thank you."

Alex shrugged.

We said our good nights.

I moved up the stairs slowly, partly to emphasize the fact that I wasn't well but also because I was more than a little unsteady on my feet. About halfway up, I stole a look back into the lounge. Everyone was eating, forking ragged chunks of fish onto the crackers and pouring water into glasses.

As soon as I stepped into my room and closed the door behind me, I started to shake. Not just slight tremors, full-on shudders. Panic hit me, and for a few seconds, I was convinced my heart was going to explode. I removed my knife and placed it on the dresser then sat on the edge of the bed and willed the attack to subside.

It did, eventually, but my hands were still shaking. I felt sick to my stomach. My carefully protected life was unraveling, and I could feel the shadow pulling at the threads, helping them along.

I lay down and closed my eyes, but sleep eluded me. I could hear the intruders talking downstairs. At least, there was a muffled scattering of words that maddeningly stayed just beyond the reach of my understanding. I tried to console myself that if they were talking about me, they were doing a poor job of making sure I couldn't hear them. But then the voices would fade to almost nothing, and I'd be left wondering whether it was a natural lull in the conversation or they'd lowered them to discuss me. As the light outside dimmed, draping the lodge in darkness, I began to wonder if they were ever going to go to bed.

Finally, I heard the rattle of plates and the shuffle of people moving around. Fresh worries played at the edges of my mind. Maybe they'd moved to the kitchen to be sure I wouldn't overhear them and were now discussing how to murder me in my sleep before *I* attacked *them*.

The shadow whispered to me—I should take the initiative, kill them first. I fought against it. I was outnumbered. All I had to do was wait a couple more days, and then they would go of their own free will. They'd promised, and they were good people.

Were they?

Clearly, Alex was hiding something, and Lucy was afraid of more than just the living dead. Ever since I was a child, I've embraced the darkness that others shy away from, and it's given me a unique perspective. I knew these people were guilty, and they were the perfect subjects for my work. I didn't need the shadow to show me that.

The wooden staircase creaked, and a few seconds later footsteps passed my door. Alex whispered a good night. Lucy and Mike replied. The doors to the other two bedrooms opened, almost in time with each other, then clicked shut. I could just about make out the sound of a lock clicking, probably from the third room. Assuming Lucy and Mike were together, they'd almost certainly chosen that one. Which meant they were concerned about safety, even if Alex wasn't.

I listened to the muffled sounds of three people getting ready for bed and hoped sleep would come to me quickly.

***

The shadow was still waiting for me when my eyes snapped open a few hours later. An iron band tightened around my chest. I sat up, each breath an effort of will. The bedclothes were drenched with sweat, and my hands were shaking. I clenched them together as though I were praying and willed them to stop.

My head was thick, my thoughts slow. A shadow in the corner of the room caught my eye, threatening to trigger another panic attack until I realized it was just the chair. The tattered remnants of a dream still clung to my mind. Images of Lucy and Mike interrogating me, dunking my head into a bucket of ice-cold water again and again until I confessed my sins.

Fueled by a potent mix of hunger and fear, my stomach twisted and rolled. Why had I let them stay? I could have refused and insisted they find their own sanctuary. Anger flared, displacing the fear. What right did they have to challenge me? They were guests in my home. I'd welcomed them, shared my food.

The shadow reared up again. Alex would be an easy target. I could picture him clearly. He'd be sprawled across the bed on his back, so deeply asleep that I'd easily be able to slide the knife across his throat. He might wake up, but it would be over before he knew what was happening.

Lucy and Mike would be harder. The door was locked, but maybe the knife could solve that problem, too. They'd be lying in bed in each other's arms, naked perhaps. I'd take Mike first but quickly enough that Lucy would be dead before she had time to react. If something went wrong and either of them woke before I was finished, I could handle them. Mike was still weak from the fever, and I was bigger than Lucy. I could overpower them both.

But part of me knew that wasn't true, and there were too many ways it could go wrong. I'd be taking an unnecessary risk. I just needed to wait them out. I dug my nails into the backs of my hands. Pain flared, a pinpoint of clarity in the haze of emotion. I pressed harder and felt the shadow recede. But it was still there, urging me to act.

The skies were clear, and the light from the moon was bathing the dresser in a pale glow and revealing my knife in all its lethal glory as though the heavens themselves were conspiring against me. The knife called to me, adding its own seductive voice to the shadow's. My head was pounding, the pressure inside building until I felt it might actually explode.

I rolled to the side of the bed and sat up. I had to do something to release that pressure, or I was going to get myself caught.

Chapter 22

RELIEF

I clutched my knife as I picked my way along the trail to the workshop. The path was dark and treacherous. The moon provided some light, but the plants and trees that cloaked the trail in the day worked to make it all but impassable at night. Again and again, I stumbled on a rock or an outstretched root. Branches clawed at my face, threatening to blind me.

Even without nature impeding my progress, the darkness provided more than adequate cover for the living dead. I'd never seen any indication that they slept at night. I could literally walk into the arms of one and not know it was there until its teeth were clamped around my throat.

But I pushed on. Every step I took toward the workshop eased the pressure in my skull. The shadow was still there, urging me on, but now we were working together. I hacked at the undergrowth blocking my way, my knife singing through the air, as eager as I was to get to our destination.

As the workshop came into view, I felt a rush of excitement. I slipped the knife back into its sheath and went inside. My snare was hanging on the wall, waiting for me.

The excitement flared stronger as I unhooked it and headed out the back of the workshop. Bones crunched beneath my feet as I walked heedlessly over the remains of the fire.

Conscious that the others might wake and find me missing, I moved as quickly as I dared. I'd spent some time out behind the workshop, but in the dark, the shadows turned the forest into an alien landscape. I picked my way past the tree hung with chains and found a narrow trail that I vaguely knew.

I'd barely made it thirty feet before I found my prey. He was short but thin, probably in his thirties, and his Hell's Angels leathers hung loosely on his emaciated form. He was stumbling through the forest, making so much noise he didn't hear me walking up behind him. It wasn't until I dropped the snare over his head that he realized anything was wrong. He twisted around as I tightened the noose, moaning urgently.

Part of his jaw was missing, and maggots cascaded from the wound as he ground his remaining teeth together. I gave a little tug, and he stumbled toward me, his groans sounding more annoyed than threatening. I tightened the noose, and he grunted. He reached instinctively for his throat, clawing at the rope but doing little more than scraping shreds of his own flesh away. I tugged the noose, getting his attention, and then led him back through the forest.

Biker Guy was surprisingly docile. It wasn't until I got him inside the workshop that he put up any resistance. Maybe he could sense what had happened to others of his kind. Perhaps their spirits still hung around the workshop.

The moment I lit the lamp hanging from the ceiling just inside the door, he started thrashing and moaning. I pulled on the snare, dragging him across the room. He was smaller than me, and lighter, and it didn't take long for me to get him into position beside the workbench. This was always the most difficult part of the operation—the transition from snare to table. I'd gotten better at it, but it was still a bit hit-and-miss.

I shoved Biker Guy backward. His legs caught the side of the table, but he immediately twisted, swinging his arms up in an attempt to dislodge the snare. I tightened my grip on the pole and pushed again. This time, he fell back onto the workbench. Still holding the noose in place, I circled around and threw the first chain across his neck.

He managed to sit up. I rammed one of the snare's blades into his shoulder and forced him back down. He let out a scream that sounded like someone grinding rock with a cheese grater. He reached for me. Clawed fingers clutched at my face as I pulled the chain tight across his neck. It took a couple of attempts to get it fed through the bracket. Not for the first time, I wondered if I might someday find someone with the same proclivities as me that could act as my assistant.

With the zombie strapped down, the rest of the task was a little easier. He kicked and thrashed as I draped the second chain across his legs, and again when I secured the third around his waist, but it was fruitless.

Once the chains were in place, I could relax and savor the moment. I removed the snare and hung it on the wall. Biker Guy twisted and moaned. I stood over him, watching his struggles gradually fade to nothing, taking my fears and worries with them. The presence of the intruders seemed less important. Now that Mike was well, I could ask them to leave, maybe even *make* them leave. Either way, they'd be gone soon, and my life could return to normal. The biker moaned, sending out a wave of fetid air and bringing me back to reality.

I went around the workshop and lit the rest of the lamps, bathing the room in a cold but oddly comforting white light. He watched me as I moved. The bones in his neck cracked as he strained to keep me in view.

I crouched down beside the workbench. Biker Guy groaned and snapped at me, the remains of his jaw flapping just inches from my face. Another wave of excitement swept through me as he strained against the chains. I stared into the black pits of his eyes and smiled.

The shadow whispered in my ear.

It was time.

I walked over to the bench beneath the windows. I didn't doubt for an instant that the leather case would still be there. It was waiting for me. I hesitated with my hand on the drawer, building the anticipation once more, then slid it open.

The case was just as I'd left it. I lifted it out and placed it gently onto the table. Then I removed a piece of cloth from the drawer—a square cut from one of the T-shirts I'd found at the camp. It was mostly white, but there were some black stains smeared across it. I smoothed out the cloth and put it next to the case. Biker Guy let out a low-pitched growl. Chains rattled. I lined the case up with the edge of the table before closing the drawer.

I ran my fingers over the case's soft leather. A stillness came over me, bringing the shadow with it. I took four deep breaths, drawing the case's energy inside my chest. I flicked my fingertips lightly over the catch and opened it.

Five scalpels. Old friends.

I traced a Z across the handles, repeating the motion until one of them, the center one, spoke to me. I slipped it out and closed the case's lid. The moonlight reflected off the blade. Behind me, the zombie moaned again. Did he know what was happening? On some primal level, maybe?

A normal person might have considered that possibility longer. They'd pause to consider the ethics of the situation. I didn't.

I picked up the piece of cloth and walked back to the workbench, covering the distance in four steps. The closer I got, the more the zombie struggled against the chains. He snapped and snarled. Blackish saliva dribbled from his chin and splattered across the floor.

I pressed the scalpel's handle against my lips as though I were kissing it. "Shhh..."

Biker Guy lunged at me. The chain around his neck shifted but held firm.

I unzipped his leather jacket and pulled it apart to reveal a black T-shirt with a picture of the devil on it. I smiled at the imagery—he'd met a new devil now.

The scalpel made light work of the T-shirt. The blade sliced through the cotton so smoothly, I could barely tell it was there. I pulled the shirt open to reveal the zombie's emaciated chest. The skin was tanned, but patches were turning gray. He'd stopped moving now and was watching me with dead eyes.

I took four deep breaths. I'd grown used to the stench of decay filling the room, but still the air was bitter, and it caught in my throat. I put my hand on the zombie's chest, a few inches in from the left-hand side, and set the shadow free.

Time stopped.

The shadow rushed through me, filling my body utterly. The workshop, the benches, the outside world were all wiped away until scalpel and zombie were the only things left.

My heart slowed. The fear that had brought me to the workshop was gone. The zombie groaned again, but the sound was distant and muffled. I could see his guilt now. Dark threads permeated his body. Black liquid poured from his mouth and ears and streamed over the edge of the table like a waterfall of oil. I could smell it, too—a bitter, metallic tang in the dusty air.

The shadow surged, and I was infused with a purity of purpose I'd never find on my own. I raised my hands toward the ceiling, tipped my head back, and let the shadow's will embrace me.

Chapter 23

AFTERMATH

I don't know how much time passed before the feeling disappeared. It felt like days, but it could only have been a few minutes. The world quickly returned to its normal, banal self. I resisted, clinging to the last vestiges of the shadow's energy for as long as I could. But eventually, there was nothing to hold on to.

An overwhelming sense of loss permeated my soul, but I felt calmer. My fears, though still there, were somehow diminished. The threat of the intruders felt manageable. They had no proof of what I really was and no real reason to go looking for it. Mike was nearly well enough for them to leave. Another day, two at most, and everything would be back to normal. I allowed myself a slight smile.

The zombie moaned, straining against the chains. The shadow had made four neat slashes across his chest. The flesh was pulled back to reveal his rotten, guilt-sodden core. His heart was missing. My hands were covered with thick black blood. More of it soaked the table and pooled on the floor. The creature held no interest to me now. It was nothing more than meat.

I took my hunting knife and rammed it into the base of the zombie's skull. He kicked and twitched for a moment and then fell still. I removed the blade and wiped it on his shirt before slipping it back into its sheath. I wanted to deal with the zombie's remains, but the eastern sky was beginning to lighten. There was no telling how early Lucy and the others would wake up, and I didn't want to push my luck. I could come back and get rid of the body later. Once they'd gone for good.

I picked up the scalpel, wiped it with the square of T-shirt, and clipped it into the leather case with the others. I hated leaving them in the workshop, but I couldn't take them back to the lodge now. It was too risky. One of the others might find it. I counted to four then snapped the lid shut, checked the catch was still working properly, and slipped the case into the drawer. The blood-soaked cloth went into a metal drum. It was too dirty to use again, and there were plenty more where that came from.

The smell from the corpse had grown stronger already. Again, I considered disposing of it straightaway. I certainly couldn't just leave it lying around for long—the smell would attract creatures from miles around, living or dead. I normally dumped the remains of my subjects in the forest, but I didn't have time to do that now.

I did a final check of the workshop then went outside. The sun had risen. It was still low in the sky, but the journey back through the forest would be less hazardous now that I could see where I was going.

I closed the door behind me and began making my way back toward the trail.

Then Alex stepped out of the forest.

Chapter 24
FAR ENOUGH

"Hey!" Alex said. "You're up early."

A cold dread ran through my veins, and the confidence that I'd felt mere seconds earlier evaporated. "Hi... yeah... I couldn't sleep."

Alex smiled. "Me neither." He looked past me at the workshop. "More of the camp?"

I took a few steps toward him, blocking his path. "Could be, yeah. I think it's a lot older, though." My throat was dry, and the words came out fractured.

"Anything interesting in there?"

"Not really."

I moved forward again. I was hoping to push him back toward the path and the camp, but he held his ground.

Alex frowned as he peered through the window. "There's some tools and stuff, though. Could be useful for something."

"Everything's rusted. The whole place is rotten. The rain probably got in during the winter."

Alex shrugged. "Maybe we can salvage something. Mike's pretty good with his hands."

The shadow twitched.

"Maybe later. It's not safe in there."

Alex scratched his chin, nodding, but he was still frowning.

I moved my hand toward my knife. As my fingers touched the leather grip, Lucy's voice called out. "Alex!"

We turned and ran through the forest, Lucy's voice pulling us along the trail. When we broke out of the undergrowth into the clearing behind the lodge, she was standing beside the back door. She slumped with relief when she saw us. When she saw Alex, anyway.

"What's the matter?" Alex said.

Lucy let out a long breath.

Mike appeared in the doorway behind her. "You'd better take a look at this."

He led us through the lodge and out onto the walkway at the front. We both looked around the camp, searching for whatever had caused Lucy's distress. It wasn't until she joined us and Mike swung the lodge door closed that I spotted it. A moment later, Alex gasped.

A hand hung from the door.

It had been hacked off just above the wrist, leaving a few tattered shreds of flesh hanging from exposed bone. By the look of the ragged nails and gray skin, it had recently belonged to a zombie. A single nail hammered through the palm attached it to the door.

Alex squinted at it. "What the...?"

Mike's lips were drawn into a tight thin line. Lucy was standing next to him. The shadow could feel the anger radiating off her.

I made an educated guess. "This has something to do with the person you've been watching out for."

Surprise flickered across Lucy's face. "How—"

A sound like a screaming, chattering monkey cut her off. It came from somewhere in the forest behind us. When I looked, I saw a man standing in the shadows.

Lucy set off toward him. "Charles!"

"Lucy, wait!" Mike said. He tried to grab her, but she twisted away from him and was gone.

The figure stepped out of the forest.

Lucy slid to a stop. "No!"

It was a zombie.

Two more shapes loomed up out of the shadows behind it. Their shuffling, uneven movements marked them as zombies, too.

Lucy pulled out her knife.

One zombie moaned and reached toward her. His right hand was missing.

Lucy let out a scream of frustration and charged at him. Mike brushed past me as he ran toward her. She collided with the zombie, and he fell backward, but she stayed on her feet. She was already kicking him before he hit the ground. Her boot hit his thigh then his ribs. Bones cracked. She raised her foot and slammed it down on the zombie's face. His skull shattered. Blood and brain sprayed across the ground.

"Look out!" Mike said.

One of the other zombies had reached Lucy. She ducked under his clumsy grab for her and swung her knife upward into his jaw. His head was forced back. Black blood poured over Lucy's hand. She yanked the knife free, and the zombie crumpled to the ground.

Mike reached her, but she waved him away. "It's mine."

The last zombie was slower. Lucy lowered herself into a fighter's stance. The zombie staggered toward her.

She screamed at him. "Come on!"

The zombie responded with a wet, gargling sound as though he was trying to speak. Lucy leaped forward and drove the knife into his forehead. He staggered back, and the movement pulled the weapon from her hand. She slammed her hands against his chest, and he toppled backward, landing with a dull thump. Lucy wiped her hands on the zombie's shirt and then tugged the knife free from his skull.

She straightened up and looked out into the trees. "This has gone far enough, Charles! Leave us the hell alone!"

When she turned back toward the lodge, her face was stony. There was a splash of black fluid across her chin. Mike tried to touch her shoulder as she passed, but she shrugged him away.

Alex and I stepped aside. She strode past and ripped the hand from the door. Then she turned and hurled it away into the forest before storming into the lodge.

Mike appeared beside us. His face was filled with concern.

"You need to tell me what's happening," I said.

He nodded. "I'll explain inside."

Chapter 25

SLICES OF THE PAST

Mike sat on the edge of couch, his hands clasped together, forefingers tapping his lips. Lucy was beside him, staring at the fireplace. Even in the dim, early-morning light, she looked pale. The anger I'd seen outside had dissipated. Now she just looked exceptionally tired. The zombie's blood was still spattered across her chin. I'd taken one of the armchairs, and Alex sat in the other. We were all waiting for Mike to speak.

Eventually, he lowered his hands and looked me in the eye. "You're right. We have been watching out for someone. His name's Charles. He used to be part of the group." He glanced toward Lucy. "But there was a difference of opinion when it came to who made the decisions."

"Between you and him?"

Mike nodded. "The plague had taken its toll on him. He became... unstable."

Alex let out a snort. "That's an understatement."

Lucy glared at him. "It's not his fault."

"I'm sorry," Alex said, raising his hands.

Mike rested a hand on Lucy's knee, and she relaxed a little.

"Five days ago, things came to a head. We argued, and he lost his temper. He came at me with a knife. I disarmed him, and I thought I had things under control. I didn't. He sucker-punched me."

"That's how you got hurt, both of you," I said, gesturing toward Alex.

"Yes. He knocked me over, and I hit my head on a rock. Alex grazed his knuckles trying to stop him."

"What happened to him?"

"He ran," Lucy said. "We thought he'd gone south, so we went north, but that night, we heard... sounds. They were just barks and screeches, things like that. We thought it might be the sound of animals in the forest, but the next day, the noises followed us as we moved."

"Had you heard them since you got here?"

Lucy shook her head.

"But you knew he was out there?"

"Not for sure, no."

I rubbed my forehead, trying to ease the pressure that was building there. "Why didn't you tell me?"

She grimaced. "We needed shelter. I was afraid that if I told you about Charles, you'd make us leave. Mike might have died if we hadn't stayed here."

Lucy was right: I wouldn't have let them stay. I had to admit, under the circumstances I would have probably done the same as her. But they didn't need to know that. The rules had changed, and I had a good reason for them to leave. I was about to tell them that when a sound from outside interrupted me.

It was a man. The words were unintelligible at first then

coalesced into fragments and finally sentences. He wanted everyone to come outside—before he burned the lodge down.

Chapter 26

CHARLES

Mike and Lucy ran to the window.

"It's Charles," Mike said.

"Aw, crap," Alex said. "I'll find the rifle."

Alex ran toward the kitchen. I joined Mike and Lucy.

A man in dirty jeans and a worn denim jacket stood at the edge of the camp, close to the path leading to the river. He was holding a flaming torch, the flickering yellow light illuminating his face and sending shadows dancing across the forest behind him. I couldn't see him well, but from here, he looked pretty normal. But then again, so did I.

"What's he doing?" I said.

Mike shook his head. "I don't know."

Charles took a few steps forward, sweeping the torch in front of him. "Come on, Lucy. I'm losing my patience." He spat Lucy's name, the words punctuated with anger.

"We need to go out there," Lucy said.

"No!" Mike said.

Charles moved farther into the camp, swinging the flaming torch around his head. "I'm going to count to five. Then this little love nest of yours goes up in flames."

Lucy moved to go outside, but Mike put his hand on her shoulder. "Luce…"

She pulled away from him, eyes blazing. "This is my fault; I'll deal with it." She turned and opened the door.

"Lucy!" Mike said. He followed her outside.

She walked out of the lodge, arms wide. "Okay, Charles, I'm here now."

Charles lowered the torch. But when he spoke, he was still angry. "Thank you."

Lucy stopped a few feet away from the front of the lodge.

When Mike appeared, Charles raised the torch again, pointing it at him. The flames flickered and sputtered, and a few drops of fire tumbled from the torch's tip onto the ground.

When Charles spoke, his voice was laden with contempt. "And here's your true love."

Mike put his hands out, palms raised toward Charles. "We don't want any trouble."

There was no sign of Alex, but if I could find the rifle, then maybe I could shoot Charles while he was distracted. I dismissed the idea immediately—I was as likely to hit myself as him.

Then again, his arrival might be a good thing. Maybe he'd solve my problem for me.

"What do you want, Charles?" Lucy said.

"You *know* what I want, Lucy."

She ran her hands through her hair. "I'm sorry, I can't give you that."

His voice rose in pitch. "So, you thought you'd kill me instead! Is that it?"

"We're not trying to hurt you! You're like a brother to me."

Charles paced left and right, an unpredictable bundle of nervous energy. "You expect me to believe that?"

"You're the one following us," Mike said. "You can go anywhere you like; we'd never find you."

Charles tapped his forehead, his face contorted in anger. "You think I don't know what you're doing? Trying to trick me."

He ran a hand through his hair. Its back was stained red. Blood.

"Charles..." Lucy said. "What did you do to your hand?"

Charles held his hand up in front of his face. He tilted his head to one side and turned his hand around, examining it. As he lowered it again, he grinned and shrugged.

"Charles, what happened?" Lucy said.

He shrugged again.

"Tell us!" Mike said. He started forward.

Charles reached behind his back, and when he brought it out again, he was holding a pistol. The gun hung limply in his hand as he waved it in Mike's general direction. "Don't."

Any temptation to let events play out deserted me. Yes, Charles might have taken care of the intruders, but then I'd have been left to deal with him. There was only room for one mentally unstable person in Camp Redfern.

I ran through the dining room and out into the clearing at the back of the lodge. I turned left and ran around the building. I could hear Charles shouting at Lucy and Mike. His voice was getting louder, more aggressive. If he really was going to shoot someone or burn the camp down, he'd do it soon.

Staying low, I ran across the gap between the lodge and Cabin Two and then made my way to the front of the building. I peeked my head around the corner. Charles had moved forward into the camp, forcing Lucy and Mike back up to the walkway. He was still brandishing the gun, waving it around, his finger on the trigger.

Mike had his hands out in front of him. He was trying to calm Charles down. "Look, why don't you put the gun away. You can come inside; we have food."

Charles jerked the gun toward Mike. "Yeah, why don't I do that. Then you can poison me."

Lucy flinched. "Please," she said, her voice filled with anguish.

I slipped the knife from its sheath and tried to gauge how long it would take me to get to Charles and whether it would be enough time for him to turn around and shoot me. Mike and Lucy were still focused on him and hadn't noticed me.

"No! You come with me, and lover boy here can go."

"She's staying right here," Mike said.

Lucy turned to him, but he shook his head.

Charles settled the gun on Mike, his aim suddenly rock solid. "I won't ask again."

There was movement on the opposite side of the lodge. It was Alex, and he was carrying the rifle. He raised it hesitantly to his shoulder and stepped out from behind the building. Before he could speak, Charles saw him and fired.

I ran at Charles. He fired toward the lodge. Lucy dodged into the cabin, wood exploding above her head. Mike ducked then ran toward Charles, who let off another shot, this one shattering the lodge's window.

I reached Charles, the knife held out in front of me. I collided with him, sending us both to the ground. The knife met resistance, and something warm and wet flooded over my hand. Charles screamed and swept the butt of his gun toward my head. It caught my shoulder, sending a jarring pain down my arm.

I leaned on the knife, pushing past the resistance. Charles screamed again. I felt the cold metal of the gun's barrel pressed against my head and realized, too late, that I'd made a terrible mistake.

The shot never came.

Instead, Mike's heavy boot stamped down on Charles's arm, snapping it. I pulled the knife out of Charles's stomach and swung it toward his neck. It sank into the soft flesh. Blood sprayed across the dusty ground. I leaned into the blade, driving it deeper. Energy flowed through me as the shadow burst to life.

Barely conscious of what I was doing, I twisted the knife and pulled, tearing it free of Charles's throat. His head rolled back. I brought the knife down, plunging it into his chest. Again and again, I struck. Blood spattered my hands, my chest, my face. The shadow screamed with joy, its excitement sending power coursing through my veins.

Eventually, I slowed my attack then stopped. My heart pounding in my head, I stood. I towered over Charles, staring down at his mutilated body, the knife clenched in my hand. Blood dripped from the blade's tip, falling in slow motion to spatter the ground at my feet. More blood pooled around the body, a vibrant crimson lake.

The shadow sang to me.

Chapter 27

AFTER THE KILL

I slowly became aware of the screaming. Just a whisper at first, tickling the periphery of my senses. A gnat buzzing in my ear. As my breathing slowed, and my heart along with it, the noise grew louder. It was joined by another sound, words that somehow I knew but couldn't pin a meaning to. And then someone touched my shoulder, and the world came rushing back.

Lucy was screaming.

Mike was holding her, pushing her shuddering form away from Charles's body. Away from me.

Alex was standing beside me, his hand gripping my shoulder. He was unhurt. Charles's shot had gone wide.

"What the hell?" Alex said. "What did you do?"

I turned toward him and raised the knife. A trickle of scarlet ran down my wrist.

Alex grabbed his mouth and whirled around. He made it a couple of steps before he lost control. Bending over, arms wrapped around his stomach, he threw up.

"Lucy! Get inside, now," Mike said.

He was trying to push her toward the lodge, but she

twisted against his grip. She kept shaking her head and saying, "He's not dead, he's not dead!" as though repeating the words would make it true.

Mike looked over his shoulder at me. His eyes were cold and filled with suspicion. The shadow retreated, returning to the depths of my psyche now that its work was done.

"Alex! Get over here," Mike said.

Alex raised his hand and spat a fresh gobbet of vomit onto the ground. I went to move toward the lodge, but Mike pointed at me. "No, Marcus. You stay right there. Don't take one step, or so help me God, I'll make you regret it."

I nodded as though I understood where the rage was coming from and why Lucy cared so much about the death of a man who until a few seconds ago had been trying to shoot her. I contented myself with wiping the knife on the ground. All I managed to do was coat the blood-soaked blade with a layer of fine brown dust. I used the leg of Charles's jeans instead.

Alex walked past me toward the lodge. Vomit flecked the front of his T-shirt. His eyes were filled with distrust. Together, Mike and Alex managed to quiet Lucy and get her inside.

When Mike came back out of the lodge, he was carrying Charles's gun. He held it loosely by his side, but the message was clear. I slipped my knife back into its sheath.

"You okay?" Mike said. His tone was quiet, tense.

"A few bumps and bruises but otherwise, yeah. I'm fine."

"That's not what I meant."

He stopped a few feet away from me, too far away for me to get to him before he could shoot me.

"What do you mean?"

Mike waved the gun toward the body at my feet. "It seemed like you got caught up in the moment there."

I looked down at Charles, the ragged slash of blood and flesh where his throat had been, the scarlet mass of tissue that was all that remained of his chest. I felt more alive than I had for months.

"I... had to stop him." I tried to lace the words with remorse but couldn't.

Mike shook his head. "There was more to it than that. There's more to *you* than that."

I looked at him and shrugged. "I don't know what to say, Mike. I was trying to stop him from killing you. Or Lucy. I didn't know what else to do."

His eyes narrowed, but whatever he was about to say was interrupted by the lodge door bursting open. Lucy stormed out, Alex close behind.

"Just let me go," she said.

When she saw Charles's body again she clamped a hand over her mouth and turned aside. She half walked, half ran across the campsite onto the path leading to the river.

Alex moved to follow her, but Mike stopped him. "She needs some time."

Alex's gaze moved to the body. "Yeah, yeah..."

I watched Lucy until she disappeared out of sight then turned back to Mike. "What aren't you telling me?"

Mike stared at me for what felt like minutes before he answered.

"We met Lucy and Charles four days after we left Seattle. They'd seen... a lot of bad stuff. Really bad stuff. Lucy never talks about it, but whatever happened, Charles felt he was responsible. He said he needed to redeem himself and became obsessed with finding a way to make it up to her. They'd been friends for years, but he was in love with her.

"As we traveled, Lucy and I became increasingly close. Charles confessed his own feelings to her, but she didn't feel the same way. After she told him, he became sullen and withdrawn. Eventually, he turned on me.

"He accused me of working behind his back to turn Lucy against him. We argued for days. The tension in the group became almost unbearable. He got more and more paranoid. Eventually, he decided I was trying to kill him. I tried to reason with him, but he attacked me, and we fought. You know the rest."

The story sounded plausible, but I couldn't be sure. Sarcasm, lies, truth, passion, they all sound pretty much the same to me. But I couldn't think of any reason for him to lie about this. I needed to stay on the group's good side, at least for now. Accusing Mike of trying to deceive me wouldn't get them out of the camp any quicker.

I nodded. "Thank you."

"Thanks for saving us, man," Alex said.

"You'd have done the same."

Neither of them responded. They didn't need to. We all knew they wouldn't have. Not in the way I had, anyway.

Mike looked down at the dead man and the pool of blood soaking into the dirt around him. "We should bury him in the forest."

"What about Luce?" Alex said.

"She blames herself for what happened, but she'll be okay. She's more than capable of looking after herself." He gestured toward the bloody remains. "But I don't want her to see this again."

We found a small clearing where the ground was reasonably soft. There were only two shovels, so one person rested while the other two dug. Even working together, it took well over an hour to get the body buried deep enough to be safe from inquisitive animals.

Alex threw the last shovelful of dirt onto the grave and

patted it down. Mike looked up into the sky at the sun. "We should go and find Lucy."

We started back toward the lodge. Mike placed his hand on my shoulder, pinning me in place. When Alex was a few feet ahead, he said, "We'll continue our discussion later."

I forced a smile. "Sure. Whenever you want."

Chapter 28

AT THE EDGE OF THE RIVER

Lucy was sitting on the rocks by the river, close to where I'd been standing when I saw the bear. Her legs were pulled up, and her arms wrapped around them. She was staring into the water.

I hung back with Alex while Mike went to talk to her.

Alex pointed his thumb over his shoulder, back toward the camp. "What you did there? That was a good thing."

The comment took me by surprise. "Really?"

"Hell yeah. I know he was Lucy's friend, but he'd lost it, man. Completely paranoid. And I mean completely. Some of the stuff he thought we were doing... crazy. You did what needed to be done."

"I don't think Lucy and Mike agree."

Alex scratched at the tangle of beard under his chin. "Mike knows, believe me. Lucy will come around. There was nothing we could do. It was him or us."

Mike reached Lucy and slipped his arm around her shoulder. She stiffened and tried to pull away from him. He spoke something, too quiet for us to hear, and she melted. She leaned into him, pressing her face against his shoulder.

"Mike doesn't trust me."

Alex gave a little laugh. "Don't take it personally. He doesn't trust anyone. It's the cop in him."

An eagle swept past, gliding low over the river. Lucy raised her head to look at it. Mike said something to her again. She drew herself upright then looked over at me. I tried to hold her gaze, but the pain in her eyes hit me unexpectedly hard. It was as real as a slap to the face. I swallowed and turned away, following the bird as it climbed up over the forest. When I looked back, Lucy was talking to Mike. I couldn't hear the words, but her body was tense, angry.

"Awww, crap," Alex said. He pointed off toward the forest. It took me a few seconds to find what had caught his attention.

It was the young man I'd seen when I'd first arrived at the river. Or it had been. He was now one of the living dead. One shoulder of his jacket had been ripped away. The exposed flesh was torn to shreds. Most of his right side was stained with blood. His right arm hung uselessly by his side. The rest of him seemed intact. Even his face was almost normal. Only the grayish tinge to his flesh and the thick black rings around his eyes betrayed the reality of the situation.

He lurched unsteadily across the rocks toward Mike and Lucy. His progress was slow but relentless.

"Mike!" Alex said.

Mike and Lucy looked around. Alex jabbed his finger toward the oncoming zombie. Mike stood, helping Lucy to her feet. He directed her toward Alex and me then reached around and calmly removed his knife from his belt. He dropped into a slight crouch and waited as the zombie came at him.

Lucy backed away a few feet then stopped. Her hands were clenched into fists.

The zombie was almost on top of Mike when he struck.

He raised the knife, and I shouted, "No!"

I was too late. The blade sank into the side of the zombie's skull. He made a halfhearted lunge for Mike. Then his legs gave way, and he collapsed to the ground. The shadow tightened inside me, and I felt an unexpected pang of loss, of an opportunity missed.

Mike joined Lucy, and together they walked over to us.

"I'm sorry," I said as Lucy reached me, contorting my face into what I hoped was a look of contrition.

She ignored me and brushed past. Alex waited for a moment then followed behind at a discreet distance.

"What did you mean? No?"

It was Mike. The knife was back in his belt, along with Charles's gun, but his brow was furrowed.

"I... I knew him. Sort of. I thought he might be okay."

Mike raised his eyebrows. "You couldn't see the gaping wound in his shoulder."

"No... Yes, but not at first. And anyway, people get hurt in other ways, too." I gestured toward the cut on Mike's forehead.

He conceded the point, and his suspicion lessened, although it didn't disappear completely. "We should probably get back to the camp in case the shooting has attracted any more of these things."

I turned to go, but Mike placed a hand on my shoulder, stopping me. "I'd stay away from Lucy for a while. She knows it was the right thing to do, but she's not ready to admit it."

I nodded.

Mike didn't speak as we made our way back to the

camp, and I was grateful for the silence. I wasn't ready to continue our earlier conversation—I might never have been.

Alex was waiting outside the lodge when we got back. He was looking at the shattered window, appraising the damage. Mike joined him on the walkway and picked at the shards of broken glass. "Where's Lucy?"

"She's upstairs. I got the sense she wasn't really interested in talking to me. Or anyone else for that matter."

Mike gave a little nod. He pointed toward the window. "See if you can find some wood and board that up. I'll make some food."

Alex gave a mock salute. "Sure thing, Captain." He walked around the side of the lodge, toward the woodpile.

Mike frowned. "Marcus..."

I was about to ask him why he looked annoyed when he pointed toward my feet. I looked down. I was standing in the middle of the dark patch of earth where Charles had breathed his last. I flinched and took a few steps to the side. Mike shook his head and went into the lodge as I scuffed my shoes across the ground.

Wary of Mike wanting to continue our discussion, I stayed outside and wandered around the camp under the pretense of checking the perimeter. It was still intact. Apparently, Charles hadn't been too insane to avoid walking into it.

Perimeter secure, I sat in one of the chairs outside the lodge. There was still a dark smear on the door where the hand had been nailed, and a few dried spatters on the walkway. Alex was working on the broken window. He'd dragged some serviceable planks to the front of the lodge and nailed a couple of the smaller ones across the opening. The two remaining pieces were far too big. Now he was digging around inside the old metal toolbox from beside the generator.

With a look of almost childlike delight, he pulled out a small wood saw. It was short, and the blade was rusty, but it was serviceable enough. Alex propped one of the planks up against the side of the lodge and began to saw.

I could see what was going to happen almost immediately. The plank bowed as Alex pressed the saw against it. The blade skipped across the wood, barely missing his fingers. He repeated the process, being more careful, and the blade dug into the wood. A couple of minutes later, the plank was cut unevenly in half. Alex hammered the pieces into place.

A gap, roughly six inches high, ran along the bottom of the window. Alex set about cutting the final plank to size. Either he'd forgotten his near miss with the first piece, or the wood was particularly hard, but the saw slid sideways again. It skipped across the plank and sliced into Alex's hand. He yelled, dropping the saw and letting the wood fall to the ground.

He clutched his hand, his face twisted into a grimace. "Goddammit!"

He lifted his fingers and peered at the wound. His face turned pale. He grabbed his hand again, his frown deepening. Blood oozed from between his fingers.

Mike stepped out of the lodge just as I got to Alex.

"You okay?" Mike said.

"Goddamned saw slipped."

"Let me take a look," I said.

Alex held out his arm and turned away. "Is it bad?"

I lifted his hand so that I could see the damage. There was a cut across the soft part of his palm. It was bleeding profusely, but he hadn't severed anything important. His biggest concern would be tetanus.

"You'll live, but you might need stitches." I turned to Mike. "There's a medical kit in the kitchen."

Mike nodded and went back inside.

I placed Alex's fingers on either side of the wound. "Press the edges together."

He gave it a tentative squeeze.

"Harder. As hard as you can."

He whimpered but did as I'd asked.

Mike reappeared, holding the medical kit and the bottle of antiseptic. It was half-empty, but there was enough to clean the wound.

I searched through the kit, hoping to find some sort of tetanus vaccine, but if there had been one, it had already been used. I found plenty of bandages, including some small butterfly ones. There was a needle and suture thread as well, but with luck, and if Alex was careful, the bandages would be sufficient. I wouldn't need to sew the wound up.

I uncapped the bottle of antiseptic, and the vapor stung my eyes. I turned Alex's hand over. "This is going to hurt."

He closed his eyes then opened them then closed them again. When I splashed the antiseptic on the cut, he let out a scream that was going to get the attention of anything within a two-mile radius. I considered reminding him of our situation but kept my mouth shut. He was the closest thing I had to an ally in this group, and I needed to keep it that way.

Alex had calmed himself down by the time I got the butterfly bandages in place. I wrapped a cloth bandage around his hand. I was actually quite proud of the job I'd done. It was neat and tidy. If he was careful for the next couple of days and didn't pull the wound open, he wouldn't have to go through the pain of actual stitches.

I told him as much, and he nodded gratefully. His brow was covered with a thin sheen of sweat, and he looked paler than ever, but otherwise, he seemed okay. The threat of tetanus obviously hadn't occurred to him. I didn't mention it. There wasn't anything I could do anyway.

I led him inside and guided him toward a seat, playing the good doctor. Once he was settled, I told him I'd get him a drink, and he smiled.

Lucy had come back downstairs, and she was sitting next to Mike. They were leaning over the coffee table, looking at a large sheet of paper. I didn't realize what it was until Alex said, "What are you looking at, Mike?"

"It's a map," Mike said, and he looked up at me, the suspicion back in his eyes.

Chapter 29

THE MAP

After a moment's hesitation, I frowned. "A map?"

"Yes. It was in a backpack in the kitchen. I found it when I was looking for the medical kit."

Frustration radiated through me. I'd left the backpack where anyone could find it. There must have been a dozen opportunities for me to hide it, but I'd let the intruders in my sanctuary distract me and forgotten.

I ignored the waves of suspicion radiating off Mike and Lucy. "Is it useful?"

"Oh yeah, very." Mike tapped his finger on the map. I knew what he'd found without looking. "There's a ranger station north of here. If the map is accurate, the terrain's pretty rough. It will take us three or four days to get there. That helicopter we keep seeing must be holed up some-where, and the station is the most obvious choice."

My stomach did a flip. I didn't want them getting the military's attention. "We don't know who has the helicopter. There are dangerous people out there."

Mike fixed his gaze on me, and I felt a flood of discom-fort. "I think it's worth the risk. This place is pretty safe, but a military or even a civilian compound is going to be even better. There may be other survivors there. And food."

"I don't think it's a good idea, man," Alex said. "Four days is a long time. We're safe here; you said so yourself. What if we get there and the station's abandoned?"

"I think it's a risk worth taking," Mike said, and Lucy voiced her agreement.

Mike tapped another part of the map. For a moment I was afraid he'd spotted the workshop, but when I looked he was pointing at Sally's Home Comforts.

"We'll need supplies for the journey. I assume this is the store you found?"

I made a show of checking out the map, my brow furrowed. "Maybe... yes, probably. I don't recognize the name."

"How much food did you say was there?"

A sudden realization dawned on me—a solution to my problem. "Lots. There's more than enough to get you to the ranger station."

"You wouldn't come with us?"

I shook my head. "I'd rather stay here."

Lucy stared at me across the map. "That's fine with me."

"I don't know," Alex said. "Maybe I should wait with Marcus. You guys can bring the military to get us when you find them."

A knot of dread formed in my stomach, fueled by Alex's words. I was so close to getting rid of them.

I tried to think of something to say to discourage Alex, but Lucy intervened on my behalf. "I don't think Marcus likes company," she said, her words laden with ice.

"But—"

Mike cut Alex off. He was looking at me. "You should come with us, Alex. It'll be safer."

I wondered if he meant safer than staying with me.

Alex started to protest.

"Mike's right," I said. "There's safety in numbers."

"Then come with us," Alex said.

Out of the corner of my eye, I caught Lucy clenching her teeth.

I sighed, turning my reply into a confession. "I can't go out there again. It was... difficult for me. I'd rather take my chances here.'

I could see the gears turning behind Alex's eyes as he fought to find a more persuasive angle to take. In the end, he just nodded and leaned back in his chair.

"When are you going?" I said, flinching inside when I realized how eager I sounded.

"We'll make the supply run tomorrow," Mike said. He ran his finger across the map. "We can take the quad bikes along this road, load them up with supplies, and bring them back here. Marcus, you can show us the way, in case the map's not accurate."

I almost told him that no, the map was definitely right, but I caught myself in time.

"We'll come back to the lodge with you then go on to the ranger station. We'll take as much of the food as we can carry; the rest can stay here. Think of it as payment for helping us."

It wasn't a terrible idea. If it worked out and they left, I'd have supplies to last me through the winter. I struggled to find a reason for me to stay at the lodge while they went on the supply run but couldn't. I nodded.

Alex was still unsure. "What about fuel?"

"The bikes should have enough to get us there and back, but there's a gas station. We can refuel if we need to."

I shook my head. "It was destroyed by a fire."

"Maybe there's some stored nearby," Lucy said.

I started to say that there couldn't be, but her eyes told me I'd be better off keeping my mouth closed.

"We'll have to risk it," Mike said. "Worst case: we leave the bikes behind and carry what we can on foot."

"What about biters?" Alex said.

"The quad bikes will be quicker than they are. As long as we keep moving, we should be fine."

If we don't meet a swarm, I thought. I didn't mention that particular pitfall. This plan was the best way to get the camp to myself. I wasn't going to shoot holes in it.

"Okay," Mike said. "Any other questions?"

Everyone shook their heads.

At last, I could see a way out of this mess, and I had to stop myself from smiling.

Mike scooped up the map and carefully folded it. "Okay. We should get some rest. We'll leave tomorrow at dawn."

Chapter 30

HOME COMFORTS

I don't know about the others, but I didn't get much sleep. I was tense, nervous about Mike changing his mind about the trip or that Alex might decide to stay at the camp instead of heading to the ranger station when they left. I knew it wasn't really going to happen, but I was desperate for them to leave. No, I *needed* them to leave so that I could get my sanctuary back.

When I wasn't cooking up new disaster scenarios, my mind was filled with images of Charles's corpse. The jagged rip in his throat, the bloody knife in my hand.

It was the first time I had been solely responsible for a kill. The shadow had been there, of course—it always was—but my actions were my own. I'd crossed a line and opened a pathway. It was just a crack, a tiny sliver, but the shadow had grown stronger since the kill. I wasn't sure I'd ever be able to control it again. I could feel it constantly now—a low-grade, ever-present hunger that threatened to swell into a wave of blackness that would break through that crack and come crashing over me. And when it did, there would be nothing I could do.

Eventually, sleep did come for me, but when I woke the next morning, my mind was fuzzy with the remnants of a dream. Every time I reached to remember the details, it slipped away. The weight of it dragged me down, almost pinning me to the bed. Even turning over was an effort. I wanted nothing more than to lie there and let the world fall apart without me.

I waited in bed until Alex came to wake me. When he hammered on the door, I feigned bleariness and told him I'd be down shortly.

Ten minutes later, I walked downstairs. Mike and Alex were already outside, checking the quad bikes. Lucy was in the kitchen. Four small piles of supplies, food and water for the trip, lay on the table. I wondered if she'd been the one to prepare the meals and, if so, whether I should check mine for poison. The thought she might be plotting to kill me brought Charles to mind again. What if he'd been right?

Lucy barely acknowledged me. She loaded three of the piles into backpacks. Mine she left on the table.

As she walked out of the room, I said, "Lucy, I really am sorry about Charles."

She stopped in the doorway, her back to me. "I know." For a moment I thought I'd found a crack, an opening I could use to repair at least some of the damage. Then she said, "I just don't care." She walked out, not waiting for my reply.

I grabbed my backpack and dropped the supplies into it. Truth be told, I didn't care what Lucy thought of me. Not on a personal level. My interest in building bridges between us came from a desire to ease her suspicion. Her anger would make her alert. She'd be looking for me to make another mistake. I couldn't afford to let my mask slip again.

I ate a breakfast of protein bars then hung around in the

kitchen, fiddling with my pack until I heard the quad bikes start up.

Outside, Mike and Lucy were checking the bikes' storage racks. They'd tied rope around them and were strapping the backpacks in place. I handed mine to Mike. Lucy slipped the green medical kit inside hers and lifted it onto the rack. Alex was leaning against the lodge, looking pensive.

Mike had two pistols. He gave one to Lucy and kept the other for himself. I averted my eyes, pretending I hadn't noticed he didn't offer me a weapon.

Lucy checked her pack was secure one last time and climbed onto the bike. "Come on, Alex, you're riding with me."

I waited for Mike to finish checking his bike and climb on before I joined him. The topic of who should drive never came up. My only concern was that he'd want to pick up our conversation on the way to the store, but as we rolled out of the camp along the rutted track that would take us to the highway, it was obvious the engines would drown out any attempt at conversation.

Mike led the way, keeping our speed high. The trees flew by as the bike bumped and bounced over the dips and ruts in the trail. More than once, I almost lost my grip. It wasn't a great leap of the imagination to picture me falling off the seat and Lucy accelerating her bike over my head, splitting it like a zombie's skull and solving the problem of what to do with the killer in their midst once and for all. It only took half an hour to get to the highway, but by the time we did, my hands ached from gripping on so tight.

We passed a dozen or so zombies on the highway—just pockets of one or two, no swarms. As Mike had predicted, we were past them before they'd had a chance to register our existence. A couple did try to chase us. They were quicker and more coordinated than the others, but even then, there was no way they could catch us.

An hour or so later we reached Sally's Home Comforts. As we crested a hill and the remains of the gas station came into sight, Mike held up his hand and pulled over to the side of the road. Lucy stopped beside him, and they turned off their engines.

Mike pointed down toward the store. "I see two."

He was right. There was a pair of zombies standing stock still a few feet away from the entrance. I wondered if it might be the couple I'd found hanging inside, but they were both businessmen by the look of their suits. They seemed to be the only zombies in the vicinity, and they hadn't seen us.

"Now what?" Lucy said.

"You three stay here. I'll go ahead on foot and take care of them. When I give the all clear, bring the quad bikes down. Park them outside the store, close to the door."

Lucy nodded.

"Marcus," Mike said. "You'll need to drive this bike."

Alex tutted, but Lucy's elbow shut him up.

"No problem," I said.

Mike got off the bike and checked his gun and knife. When Lucy saw him keep the knife out and put the gun away, she frowned. He crouched low and ran across the road, staying close to the trees as he made his way down the hill. My heart quickened as he approached the gas station. I clenched my fists, and the palms were slick with sweat, although I couldn't tell you whose safety I was most concerned for—his or the zombies'.

We watched the zombies standing outside the store, searching for a sign that they'd seen Mike. They were almost motionless, just rocking slightly as though they were trees swaying in a breeze.

When Mike reached the gas station, he slowed down. After pausing for a couple of minutes at the edge of the blackened forecourt, he ran to the side of the building, glancing left and right as he crossed the open space. The zombies still hadn't seen him, and nothing had come lumbering out of the shadows.

They were standing next to each other, about ten feet from the entrance to the store, looking out across the road. Mike would need to go around the back of the building if he wanted to get to them without being seen. Still crouched, he crept along the side of the gas station and out of sight.

A couple of minutes later, he came sprinting out from behind the station. The knife flashed in his hand as he ran. He made it to within twenty feet of the zombies before they heard him. As one, they turned around and lurched forward. I caught sight of movement from the corner of the store, and another zombie appeared, heading straight toward Mike.

"Crap," Lucy said and flicked the ignition on her bike. The engine whined and spat then died.

Mike collided with the first zombie, driving him backward into the second. The three of them hit the ground in a tangle of limbs. Mike rolled sideways, slashing the knife upward as he moved. It flashed through the air, slicing through one of the business-zombie's arms. He ignored the wound and caught hold of Mike's leg.

Lucy's engine stuttered again, quieter this time, and she let out a groan of frustration.

Mike kicked, slamming the heel of his boot into the zombie's face. His head snapped back, but he kept hold of Mike's ankle. The second zombie had recovered enough to stagger back to his feet, and he took a handful of steps toward Mike.

I didn't react immediately. Part of me, the part the shadow had the most influence over, wanted to wait and watch.

I heard a faint voice. It took me a few seconds to realize it was Lucy shouting at me. "Marcus! Help him!"

Her words broke the shadow's grip. I slid forward on the quad bike and turned the ignition. The engine roared to life. Without thinking, I pressed the accelerator with my thumb. The engine growled, and the bike leaped forward, threatening to leave me behind. It veered dangerously toward the side of the road, kicking dirt and dust into the air.

I yanked on the handlebars. The bike skewed sideways and almost pitched me onto the asphalt before I realized I should ease up on the accelerator. The bike slowed quickly, even without me applying the brake. It was enough for me to get it straightened up and pointing roughly down the road. This time, I pressed the accelerator lever more slowly, and the quad bike steadily increased its speed.

Mike was still wrestling with the zombie businessmen. He kicked one again. His boot jarred the zombie's head sideways, snapping his neck. It hung at an unnatural angle, but the zombie still had his hand firmly clasped around Mike.

The second zombie was a couple of feet away. Mike changed his approach. He slammed the heel of his boot down onto the wrist of the creature holding him then twisted his foot sideways. The zombie loosened his grip.

Mike scrambled away from the first zombie as the second pitched forward, his hands grasping for Mike's throat. He missed but caught the back of his jacket. Mike twisted, yanking himself free of the zombie's grip.

Lucy's bike finally burst into life and accelerated down the road. Mine skipped over a bump and slid sideways.

Instinctively, I eased off the accelerator until it straightened up.

Mike was on his feet, and the zombies were advancing toward him. Behind him, the third zombie was closing in. My quad bike bounced off the road and onto the concrete apron around the gas station.

I shouted at Mike, but the zombies were keeping him busy. Lucy had left Alex at the top of the hill and was racing toward the store, but she was still at least twenty seconds away.

I considered my options. I could still let Mike die and claim I was just too late. Lucy would blame me anyway. She'd see through me no matter what I said, and she'd be angry. Probably angry enough to try to kill me. And if Mike somehow managed to fight off the zombies, I'd be making my situation worse by holding back. I needed to stick to the plan and help them so that they could leave. I accelerated toward the third zombie, scattering gravel as I went.

Both of the businessmen were back on their feet and advancing toward Mike. He swung his knife, slashing at the nearest one. The blade caught the zombie's neck. It opened up a deep gash but did little to slow him down. With his head lolling to one side on his broken neck, the other zombie lunged. Mike sidestepped the attack then charged.

The third zombie loomed up in front of me. I ducked, jerking left just as I reached him. The front right corner of the quad bike hit him. The impact tore his leg apart. He was spun around, scattering flecks of blood and bone across the ground as he fell.

I pulled on the brakes, and the bike slid to a halt in a cloud of gray dust and gravel. The engine coughed and died. I half climbed, half fell off the bike. As I scrambled back to my feet, I grabbed the knife from my belt. I took four long paces and slammed the blade into the zombie's skull before he could recover from the collision.

Mike had killed the businessman with the broken neck. He lay on the ground, Mike's knife sticking out of his skull. A pool of thick black blood lay congealing around his head. But the other zombie was still upright. He had fresh slashes across his face and neck and a puncture wound in his shoulder, but he was still advancing toward Mike.

I called to Mike and, as he turned, lobbed my knife toward him. It fell short, bouncing across the gravel and stopping a couple of feet away from him. He waited until the zombie lunged then, in one fluid movement, ducked and scooped up the knife.

He turned on the zombie, leaping toward him and driving the knife into the back of his skull. The zombie pitched forward, landing face-first on the gravel.

Mike staggered backward. He was breathing heavily, and his face was spattered with black blood, but otherwise, he seemed unharmed.

Lucy leaped off her quad bike as it slid to a stop and ran to Mike. She grabbed his shoulders, her eyes sweeping over him, searching for bites.

"I'm fine," Mike said. He'd tried to force some lightness into his voice, but the words came out uneven, afraid.

Lucy turned Mike around and inspected the rest of him then wrapped her arms around him in a bone-crushing hug. She buried her face into his neck and made a strangled sobbing sound.

Alex was almost down the hill. I waved at him to show we were okay then realized I wasn't sure we were. I moved away from the store, circling around until I could see the far side of the building, where the third zombie had come from.

The car I'd seen on my first visit was still there, and I

could see shapes moving around inside, but the doors were closed. There was no sign of any other zombies.

When I rejoined Lucy and Mike, they'd untangled themselves from each other and were moving among the corpses, driving their knives into their skulls to make sure they were dead.

"Any more?" Lucy said.

"No. It looks clear."

Alex trotted the last few feet across the forecourt. He was supporting his injured hand. "Everyone okay?"

"We're all fine," Lucy said, but her eyes were full of anger. She'd seen me hesitate when Mike was attacked.

Mike put a hand on my shoulder. "Thanks."

"Just doing my part."

He nodded, but his eyes lingered on me for a moment as though he was trying to get a handle on my behavior. Then he brushed some dust off his jeans. "Okay, let's be as quick as we can. Alex, see if you can find some more gas for the bikes. The three of us will go inside the store."

Lucy gave us each a pack. "Be careful. We don't know how many more of those things there are."

"Marcus," Mike said. "Where are the supplies?"

"In the left-hand side of the building. The right is just a restaurant. All the food in the kitchen is rotten."

"Any other rooms?"

"Yes, there's a living room, bathroom, and bedroom at the back."

"Anyone in there?" Lucy said.

"An old couple. Suicides. I didn't see anything worth taking."

"Okay, we'll hit the left side and leave the rest. There's no point spending more time here than we have to. Alex, meet us back here in ten minutes. Any problems, you run. Okay?"

Alex nodded and set off toward the remains of the gas station.

Mike led Lucy and me to the building, motioning for us to wait outside while he checked the entrance. As soon as he was through the door, Lucy followed him inside. I hovered outside for a few seconds, unsure of what to do, then went after them.

Inside, Mike was glaring at Lucy. When he saw me, he raised his eyebrows. I shrugged. Shaking his head, he pointed toward the left-hand side of the building. "Slowly."

We moved into the store, spreading out along the window so that, between us, we were covering the whole room. Everything seemed as I'd left it. Mike checked behind the counter. "All clear. Okay, stick to packets wherever possible then move on to cans. Try to get food with lots of protein. It'll keep us feeling satisfied for longer. If it tastes okay cold, even better."

We opened our backpacks and began moving through the store. My aisle had a lot of laundry detergent, magazines and tourist knickknacks, but there were half a dozen boxes of soup, some dried pasta, and a small stack of canned potatoes. I threw them into my backpack, forgetting to check the protein levels first. Even with the cans, my pack was only about a third full, so I moved on to the next aisle, the one Lucy was looting.

This one was more lucrative, and Lucy was only halfway down it. I grabbed anything that looked reasonably nutritious and put it into my pack. Lucy was being more methodical, checking ingredients as she went.

I met her at the halfway point. My pack was almost full, so I added a couple of cans of chili and went to put my haul by the bike.

I'd barely stepped outside when I heard Alex shouting. I

couldn't understand what he was saying, and it took me a couple of seconds to spot him. He was running across the apron of the gas station, arms waving. He pointed down the road, farther past the store. I turned and immediately wished he'd stop screaming.

A swarm of zombies was making their way up the hill toward us.

Chapter 31

THE SWARM

The zombies had seen us. They'd veered in the direction of the store—dozens of them lumbering up the slope. Three of them were out front. They were moving quickly, almost running up the hill and leaving the bulk of the swarm behind.

I leaned back inside the store and called out. "Mike, Lucy, you'd better get out here! Quick!"

A few seconds later, Lucy appeared at my shoulder. "Crap. Mike, there's dozens of them."

Mike took in the swarm then waved at Alex, directing him toward the quad bikes.

"Come on," he said, "we need to get out of here."

Mike reached the bikes first. He dropped his backpack onto the rack and leaped onto the seat. I added my pack to his and wrapped the rope around them. He twisted the ignition key, and the engine kicked into life. Shouting at me to get on, he revved the engine twice.

There were at least fifty zombies in the swarm, and it was still growing as even more shambled into view. The air was filled with a persistent drone—the voices of the dead.

The cluster of fast-moving zombies had grown to six now. They were less than forty feet away from Lucy's bike, and she was still strapping her backpack into place.

Alex grabbed her arm and pointed at the swarm. "Lucy, we have to go."

Lucy looked up, saw how close the zombies were, and swore. She wound the rope around the metal rack one more time then climbed onto the bike and twisted the ignition.

Nothing happened.

She tried again, turning the key so hard I thought it might snap. The engine gave a halfhearted whine then fell silent.

Alex climbed on the back of the bike, running his hands through his hair. "Come on, Lucy, they're getting close."

"I know!"

She tried the key again.

When the engine didn't respond, she looked up at Mike. "You go. Come back for us when they've gone."

Mike looked past me to the oncoming crowd of zombies. He shook his head. "No, we all go, or we all stay." He killed the engine and climbed off the bike. "Come on! Get inside."

He ushered us into the building as the first zombies reached the bikes. I could smell them—a wave of rancid air that swept before them and caught in my throat.

Mike swung the door shut. "Find something to block it."

Alex and I dragged a couple of chairs from the restaurant and wedged them under the door handle. The zombies lurched toward the building, ignoring the bikes and our supplies.

"I hope you've got a plan," I said, "because this door won't hold them for long."

"Alex, secure the restaurant. There's probably other entrances; make sure they're closed. Lucy, check the store.

Marcus, stay here in case they start breaking through. I'll take the back room."

Before I could object, they'd gone.

A solid thump came from the door. Even though I'd known the zombies were there, it still made me jump. One had thrown herself against the door. Her face was pressed against the glass, mouth twisted into a distorted grin.

Another zombie arrived, crushing the first as it fought to get at me. They jostled and bumped each other as they clawed at the door. A cut opened up in the face of the second zombie, and it left thick black smears across the glass as he fought to get at me.

"Marcus!" Mike said from behind me. He was backing out of the living room, his knife held out in front of him.

"Why didn't you kill those two while you were here? They could break free."

"It just... didn't seem right, somehow."

He shook his head, clearly not seeing my side of things. "Are there any more?"

"No, not that I know of."

He slammed the door closed behind him and rejoined me.

There were at least a dozen zombies outside now, and the bulk of the swarm would arrive within a couple of minutes. Most of them were clustered around the door, but three had spotted Lucy and were tracking her through the store window. One of the zombies at the door stumbled and fell. Two more took his place, crushing him beneath their feet.

Lucy appeared. "There's a fire exit, but it's locked tight. The window will give way before they get through it."

A few seconds later, Alex joined us in the cramped hall-way. "There's a way out through the back of the restaurant.

The door's a bit warped, but I think it'll hold if they try to get in that way."

A fist slammed against the door, rattling it in its frame.

Alex took a step back, eyeing the zombies warily. "What about the other rooms?"

"The store is secure," Mike said. "There's a couple of zombies in the living room that Marcus forgot to mention."

"What!" Lucy said.

I raised my hands. "They're not a threat, they're... tied up."

"It's okay, Luce," Mike said. "I'll take care of them."

Lucy handed him the pistol, and he went back into the living room. A few seconds later there were two hollow pops. They were quickly followed by dull thumps, presumably as Mike cut down the bodies.

"Any ideas how we're going to get out of here?" Alex said.

The swarm had well and truly arrived. Some of the tail-enders were passing by, not aware of the potential meal cornered by their compatriots, but the space in front of the store was packed three deep with living dead. And nearly all of them were trying to get at us.

One of the zombies smashed its head against the glass door, creating a blood-covered spiderweb of cracks. It started biting at the glass, trying to chew its way inside.

Mike reappeared. "The back rooms are clear." He looked out at the mass of zombies. His jaw clenched.

The swarm ignored the bikes, but that was the only thing going our way. I could see thirty or forty of them, and there could easily be more out of view. Some in the crowd were milling aimlessly around, but most were clamoring to get at us. The front row of zombies was already crushed hard against the glass door, and another group had formed by the store window. It wouldn't be long before one or the other broke through.

"We should go into the living room," I said. "Where they can't see us."

"They already know we're here," Lucy said.

"Yes, but at least we won't look like meat hanging in a butcher's window."

"He's right," Mike said. "Come on."

The old couple was lying on the floor in the middle of the living room. There was a neat bullet hole in each of their foreheads and a much less neat knife wound in the bases of their skulls. The electrical cords they'd used to hang themselves were still wrapped around their necks.

I left the living room door ajar and stood next to it, watching the zombies at the entrance.

Alex let out a breath and circled around the bodies to the window at the back of the room. "Looks like it's clear, for now."

"We need to get out of here while we still can," Lucy said.

"What if we go out the back?" I said.

"And then what?"

"We could get to the forest, head back up the road, and cross over when we're out of sight of the swarm."

"He's right," Alex said.

"What about the supplies?" Lucy said.

I shrugged. "We come back for them once they've gone."

Mike shook his head. "We have no idea when that will be, or how many of them we'll meet in the forest. For all we know, there could be more of them in the trees than out there."

I thought of my encounter with the giant swarm. He had a point, but either we ran, or we stayed in the store and waited for the zombies to break in and tear us apart. Neither option felt like a smart choice. Short of discovering a hidden cache of heavy weaponry behind the couch, we were out of options. We stood in silence, the decision hanging in the air between us.

There was a thump from outside and the sound of breaking glass. I checked the front door. Part of the upper panel had broken, and a pair of zombies were trying to drag themselves through. The shards of glass still sticking out of the door dug into their flesh, shredding it as they attempted to clamber into the building. A narrow stream of black blood trickled down the door.

"We're running out of time," I said. "We can't stay in here, and you're right about the forest. Which means our best option is the bikes."

"Which are surrounded by monsters that want to chew off our faces," Alex said.

I conceded the point then said, "So we draw them off. A couple of us go out the back and attract their attention to pull them away from the store. When it's clear, the other two grab the bikes. They can pick up the decoys on the way up the road."

Alex looked like he was going to object, but Mike got in first. "I agree. We can't stay here."

"And if the bikes don't start?" Lucy said.

"Then we go with Plan B," Mike said. "We try to make it to the forest." He looked around the room at us, waiting for someone to raise an objection.

It was Lucy who brought up the obvious question. "So, who's the bait?"

Without realizing what I was doing, I raised my hand. "I'll go."

Mike nodded once then looked at Alex.

Alex's shoulders sank. "Okay." He lifted his injured hand and waggled it. "I'd struggle to drive a bike anyway."

I checked outside. One of the zombies had wandered around the edge of the building, but it was ambling toward the forest with its back to us. "It's still clear, but I don't know for how long."

Mike held out the gun. "You should take this."

I shook my head. "Not unless Alex wants it. I'm more likely to blow my own foot off."

Alex gave a little snort of laughter. "Then we'd be competing to see who could maim themselves first. You keep it. Just make sure you get to those bikes."

"Hold on," Mike said, and he went into the bedroom.

At the front of the building, the zombies had almost made it through the broken door, but there were so many now that they were hampering each other's progress. They saw me. The low droning that seemed to hang in the hallway intensified in pitch. One of the zombies threw herself at the window. Black gore spattered the glass, and a crack formed.

Mike reappeared with a battered wooden baseball bat. "If you don't want the gun, take this."

Alex raised his injured hand, looking unhappy. "You'd better have it."

I took the scratched and worn bat. It seemed solid. "Thanks."

Lucy placed a hand on Alex's shoulder. "You ready?"

He took a deep breath and let it out, very slowly. "As ready as I'll ever be."

Mike checked the window then unbolted the door.

"You guys stay out of sight," Alex said.

Mike nodded. "Good luck."

I cracked open the door and peered out. The lone

zombie was still heading toward the forest, but I could only see half of the parking lot. I could feel the shadow's growing excitement and had to pause to gather my wits for a few seconds.

I pushed the door open and stepped into a wall of rancid air, heavy with the stench of rot and blood. A zombie reared up off to my right, his face so decayed most of the flesh had fallen away.

Chapter 32

DECOYS

I shouted and pulled back, but Alex was right behind me, and I bumped into him. The zombie was as surprised as I was at finding lunch standing right in front of him. It took a few seconds for his decaying synapses to instruct his arms to reach for me. His hand grazed my shoulder. I ducked and then darted forward before spinning around to face him.

One of the zombie's eyes was missing, torn out by something or someone. The other tracked me as he dragged himself around and came at me again. I raised my bat, but Alex ran at the zombie from out of the shadow of the store. He slammed into his back and sent him sprawling.

The zombie grabbed at my leg. I swung the bat down onto his skull. It shattered. Bits of brain and black gunk splashed across the ground. I hit him again, twice. The shadow pulsed in time with the blows.

As soon as Lucy saw we were safe, she pulled the door shut, locking us outside. Mike's face appeared in the window, his expression tense.

"Come on," I said.

"Hold on."

Alex ran across the lot and picked up a metal bar. It was rusted and bent, but it was better than nothing.

We moved around the building until we could see the swarm. Most of it was still focused on the front of the store, but a few of the zombies had given up and were wandering in random directions. One was next to an abandoned car, clawing at the rear window. Two more were simply standing in the middle of the road, staring up at the sky.

The quad bikes were intact but surrounded by zombies. The shadow tried to goad me into leaving Alex and the others behind. I pictured myself riding off up the road, supplies strapped behind me. Life would return to how it was—me living alone in the camp. I'd be free again. It was all I could manage not to run for the nearest bike.

We started shouting and waving our arms. It was odd at first, and our instinct for self-preservation naturally kept our voices low. Some of the zombies saw us and turned their attention away from the building, but most didn't.

I waved my arms again and screamed. "Come on! Over here, you ugly bastards!"

It felt like every single zombie turned to look at me, their heads moving in perfect unison. A handful, the less decayed of the group, broke away immediately and lumbered across the parking lot toward us.

Alex added his own cry, jumping up and down and waving his arms like a madman. More of the zombies began moving, and their moans intensified, filling the air.

"Now what?" Alex said.

"We get moving."

We turned and jogged back the way we'd come, still shouting, still waving our arms. More zombies peeled away from the store—a tidal wave of the living dead heading our way. Some picked their route carefully, avoiding the rocks and grass. Others were less observant, and a couple stumbled on lumps of concrete and went down. They were quickly swallowed up by the swarm. If they got back up, I didn't see them.

Alex swore. Another group of zombies had appeared ahead of us. There were a lot fewer of them, no more than ten, but they were still in our way. We slowed to a walk, moving closer to the tree line. There was still room for us to get to the bikes if we went around the gas station, but it was a lot farther than I'd have liked. I began to wonder if maybe we should have taken Mike up on his offer of a gun.

Most of the main swarm had rounded the corner now. There were just a few stragglers left bringing up the rear. I couldn't see Lucy or Mike through the living room window. With luck, the front of the store would be clear and they'd be making their way to the bikes.

A few of the faster zombies were closing in. I pointed toward the wreckage of the gas station. "We should start moving that way, try to get to the front before they cut us off."

Something cracked in the trees. A zombie in a pink floral dress stumbled into view. I backed off, drawing her out while Alex held his ground.

When the zombie was within range, Alex darted forward and drove the metal bar into the side of her head. Blood and bone and brain flew through the air, and she went down. We didn't wait to see if she got up again.

We had the zombies' attention now, and we concentrated on getting safely across the parking lot. The group ahead of us had grown; there were closer to fifteen of them now. They were clustered together. One good grenade would have taken them all out. If we'd had one.

A gunshot rang out. Two more followed in quick succession. I listened for the sound of the bikes starting up, but all I could hear was the swarm's drone. As we got closer to the gas station, two more zombies stumbled into view. They were both badly damaged, their arms crushed, torsos ripped open to reveal scarlet flesh. We ran directly at them, weapons raised.

I reached the dead first. The shadow rose up, filling me with malevolent energy. I swung my bat at the closest zombie. Wood met bone, and his jaw shattered. He staggered and fell.

Alex brought the bar down on top of the other zombie's head, shattering her skull. She fell to the ground. Alex swung the bar again and made sure she didn't get back up. I did the same, swinging my bat into the side of my zombie's head as though I were holding a golf club.

We pushed on, moving along the side of the building toward the pumps. A female zombie stumbled across the burned-out station. Her progress was hampered by the wreckage of the building's roof. I made a beeline for her, readying my bat.

Alex called out. "Marcus!"

He was pointing toward the store. Lucy and Mike had reached the bikes, but they were surrounded by a group of five zombies. We veered toward them and started shouting again.

One of the zombies, a heavily decayed specimen wearing the tattered remains of a black trench coat, staggered across the pavement in our direction. Its jaw dropped open, and it groaned. Something thick and wet fell from its mouth. The others ignored us, intent on closer prey.

Another shot rang out, and the back of one of the zombie's heads exploded. Lucy was carrying some kind of steak knife, and she swung it, ramming it into the side of another zombie. He fell back, pulling the knife out of her grip. A zombie in a hockey jersey grabbed at her, and she stumbled sideways. She flung out a fist but missed. The zombie lunged at her again. She managed to get her arm up under the creature's chin, but his momentum carried them both to the ground.

The zombie we'd distracted turned back toward Mike just as he raised his gun. He pulled the trigger, hitting the zombie in the side of the head. The bullet tore off his ear but did nothing to stop him. Mike fired again, but there was no gunshot, just a hollow click. A fraction of a second later, the zombie was on him. A second, a woman in blue jeans, grabbed him, too. He fell backward, the bike keeping him upright as he struggled with the zombies.

I pushed harder, accelerating even as my lungs cried out for air. Lucy was still trapped beneath the hockey fan when I reached her. He snapped and snarled at her, spattering her face with flecks of blood as she tried to push him away. I raised the bat, ready to hit the zombie, but he was too close to Lucy.

She let out a guttural scream and pushed him up and away from her face. I hooked the bat around his throat and pulled backward, dragging him off of her. The zombie reached back. His hands clawed at me, raking my jacket. I tightened the bat, hoping the pressure might break his neck, but my hand slipped on the blood-covered wood. He grabbed at me again, and I smelled rotting flesh as his hand brushed my face.

"Marcus!"

It was Alex. He'd pulled up a couple of feet away from

me, the bar held over his shoulder as though he was the one holding the baseball bat. I twisted around, turning the zombie toward him, then pushed.

As the zombie stepped forward, Alex swung. The bar caught him on the side of his head, and he went down.

Lucy let out a cry.

Mike had managed to get his knee between him and the zombie on top of him, but the other one had her arms wrapped around his shoulders. Only the gun wedged sideways in her mouth was stopping her from tearing him apart. I rammed the end of the bat into the trench coat–wearing zombie's face. The blow didn't kill him, but it was enough to send him staggering away from the bike. Mike rolled sideways, twisting free of the other zombie's grip.

I swung at the trench-coated zombie again. The bat crunched into the side of his head, and his skull shattered. As he fell to the ground, I turned, ready to go after the female zombie, but Lucy had retrieved her steak knife. She drove the blade into the side of the zombie's neck. The zombie screamed and tried to grab Lucy, but it was too late. She twisted the knife, unleashing a torrent of black blood from the zombie's throat. The zombie collapsed, dead.

Mike was already on the bike. He twisted the ignition key, and the machine coughed and spluttered to life.

He gunned the engine. "Come on!"

We only had one working bike.

I looked at Lucy. She ignored me, climbing onto the blue quad bike instead. Her actions confused me for a couple of seconds, then I saw the jumper cables connecting the two bikes. Mike revved the engine again as Lucy turned the ignition key. The bike whined but didn't start.

"Lucy..." Alex said.

The swarm of zombies had rounded the corner and was moving toward us.

"Nearly there," she said and tried the ignition again. The bike was silent, not even a whine.

Two more zombies appeared behind us, stragglers that had been too slow to get taken in by our diversion. I swung my bat, an uppercut that caught the nearest one beneath the jaw and sent it spinning backward.

Alex wasn't so lucky. His zombie was tall—well over six feet. He swung the bar and caught him on the shoulder. There was a crack, but he didn't slow down.

Behind us, the engine whined again. This time, it caught. Lucy let out a shout of victory.

"Go on!" I said and stepped between Alex and the tall zombie.

He reached for me, and I hit him in the chest with the bat. My arms were tired, and the blow was weak. I changed tack and smashed the bat into his right leg. His knee collapsed inward, and he pitched forward. Swinging the bat over my head, I slammed it into his back, driving him to the ground.

Not caring whether I'd actually killed him, I turned and ran toward the bikes. Alex was already sitting behind Lucy, a backpack of supplies clutched in his arms. The bandages on his hand were stained red, but it wasn't clear who the blood belonged to. Lucy revved the engine and accelerated forward. The jumper cables snapped free and bounced along behind her.

There were two more zombies half a dozen feet from the back of the other bike, both of them young boys. Mike looked over his shoulder and shouted at me to hurry. Not needing to be told twice, I grabbed a backpack that was lying on the ground then climbed on board. Mike had the bike moving before I was even sitting down, and we sped away from the zombies, spraying gravel and dirt in our wake.

The swarm had spread out, and the road was a sea of shambling, rotting corpses. Lucy was already well ahead of us, weaving through the crowd as best she could.

Her bike jerked sideways, out of the way of an oncoming zombie, but it wasn't enough. The back hit him and knocked him to the ground. The bike tipped. Lucy leaned left, righting it again. She twisted the handlebars, trying to dodge another zombie. The front fender slammed into him. His legs buckled, and Lucy's bike bounced as she ran over him. She slowed, let the bike settle, then accelerated again.

Mike pushed on, slaloming through the path Lucy had cut. As we reached the top of the hill, the swarm ahead of us thinned out. Lucy was able to slow, and by the time we were heading down the other side, we'd pulled alongside her.

Alex gave a thumbs-up, but his face was pale, and he was clutching a backpack as though his life depended on it. I checked my hands and face for cuts and bites. Mike's cheek was bruised, and there were splashes of black blood on his jacket, but otherwise, he seemed fine.

We accelerated away from the swarm. The aftereffects of the adrenaline-filled fight had left my arms and legs feeling weak. I tried to focus on not falling off as the bike raced along the highway.

I smiled. We had food now, maybe not as much as we'd hoped, but enough for Mike and the others to get to the ranger station. Enough for them to leave.

The path through the forest was nearer than I remembered, and my excitement grew as the bikes turned onto the trail that led to the camp. Within a few hours, I'd be alone again.

We were almost back at the camp when we hit the zombie.

She lurched out of the forest in front of us, just as we rode over a blind crest. Lucy swerved to miss her, and the back end of the bike slid into a drainage ditch. It slewed sideways as she twisted the handlebars, trying to stay upright. For a moment, it looked as though she'd manage it. Then the front left wheel hit a rock, and the bike bounced over the lip of the ditch and tipped sideways. It skidded to a halt in a cacophony of twisting metal and shattering plastic.

Mike and I weren't so lucky. He braked as soon as he saw the zombie, but it was too late. The bike slid forward on the loose earth and hit her head-on. The impact caught her at the knees, throwing her forward on top of the bike. She grabbed at Mike. Ragged nails tore across his cheek, and he screamed in pain.

The zombie's legs were a mass of shattered bone and torn muscle where the bike's metal grill had torn them apart. She ignored the damage and attacked Mike. Her injured legs stopped her from getting much traction, but she managed to get one hand within reach of his shoulder. She clutched it, digging in clawlike fingers and using the leverage to drag herself forward. Mike struggled with her, but with me behind him he had no room to move.

I threw myself off the bike. Mike punched at the zombie. The blow caught her on the side of the head, but as he pulled back she lunged again. Her teeth clamped around his wrist. He screamed as she tore into his flesh. Blood poured down his arm.

Pulling out my knife, I ran at the woman. She lifted her head from Mike's wrist, ripping away a chunk of flesh. I rammed the knife into the base of her neck and twisted. She screamed—a high-pitched wail that set my teeth on edge and sent the shadow into paroxysms of excitement. I stabbed at her neck again, and the screaming stopped. I shoved her away from the bike with my foot.

Mike was lying on the bike, his hand clutched around his wrist. His face was contorted in agony. Blood poured from between his fingers, soaking his jeans and the bike. He was already turning pale.

Chapter 33

THE BITTEN AND THE BROKEN

Lucy dragged herself free of the other bike and clambered out of the ditch. "Mike! Oh God, no!"

There were tears streaming down her face. Blood trickled from a cut across her forehead and turned the tears red. She grabbed Mike's face and turned it to look at her. His eyes flickered open.

"You fight it, Mike. We'll find a way to stop it spreading."

Mike shook his head slightly, and his eyes closed again.

"Marcus, we have to do something!"

I looked at the wound on his wrist and the blood still pouring from it. It was too late. "Get me the medical kit."

Mike's head tipped forward.

"Hey!" shouted Lucy. "You stay awake, or I swear I'll kill you. You hear me?"

He didn't reply. She let go and ran to get the medical kit.

I lifted Mike's arm, and he cried out.

"Sorry, but you need to keep it raised and press hard on the wound."

He groaned, but I saw him tighten his grip.

Ahead of us, the trail widened. We were only a few minutes from the camp. We could get him back to the lodge, but then what? He'd been bitten, and there was no coming back from that.

Lucy reappeared, clutching the medical kit. She opened the case and held it out to me. The contents seemed so inadequate. A few bandages, the remains of the bottle of antiseptic, a couple of squares of gauze, and some off-the-shelf painkillers. I pulled out the antiseptic and unscrewed the cap. Then I lowered Mike's arm and tipped the contents of the bottle onto the wound. The air was filled with screams and the smell of hospitals. Lucy turned her head away.

I threw the bottle aside and grabbed the bandages and gauze. "Give him the painkillers."

Lucy took the bottle and unscrewed the lid. Her hands were shaking. "How many?"

I hesitated. "As many as you like."

Anger flashed through her eyes, but she didn't speak. She tipped a few of the tablets into her hand and raised it to Mike's mouth. "Here."

He pulled his head away.

"Go on," she said, her voice cracking.

Mike relented and took the pills in his mouth. Lucy watched until she was sure he'd taken them. I think she was right—he would have spat them out if she hadn't.

The antiseptic had washed away some of the blood, but more had already taken its place. The bite was too deep. I pressed the gauze onto Mike's arm and wrapped a bandage around the wound. It immediately turned red.

"Lucy? Marcus?"

It was Alex. His voice was tight, laced with pain.

"Go and help him," I said.

Lucy placed a hand on Mike's shoulder, but he knocked it away. "Go," he said. His voice was rough, full of pain.

I wrapped the rest of the bandage around his arm, pulling it as tight as I could. Blood was still soaking through, but it did seem to be slowing. I raised his arm again.

Mike grunted in pain. "You're wasting your... time... You know what needs to be done."

I looked over at Lucy. She was knee-deep in the ditch, trying to shift the bike.

"Marcus!" Mike said. "We *all* know." The words came through gritted teeth.

He was right. I retrieved my knife from the zombie. Without thinking, I wiped the blade on the ground to clean it. Mike nodded to me.

"No!" screamed Lucy. "Don't you dare!"

She was standing back on the trail with her gun pointing at me. "If you try, I'll shoot you." The barrel of the weapon wavered but not enough for me to be sure she'd miss.

"Luce..." Mike said.

"No, Mike. I'm not going to let you die."

He fell forward until he was draped over the front of the bike. Sweat beaded his brow, and his skin was pale and waxy. He managed to raise his head to look at Lucy. "Please..."

A fresh wave of tears broke over Lucy's cheeks. I could see her fighting with herself. Mike was right; we all knew it was too late. She shook her head, and Mike's shoulders dropped. His head dipped, and his eyes closed.

"Come on, Marcus," Lucy said. "I need your help."

She waved the gun at me. I held up my hand and slipped my knife back into its sheath.

Alex was pinned by the bike. His eyes were open, but his

shirt was slick with sweat. The cut in his hand had opened up again. Blood had soaked through the bandage and into the sleeve of his jacket.

I crouched down beside him, peering beneath the bike. He tried to smile, but the movement turned into a grimace. I could see his leg was wedged between the storage rack and the ground. There wasn't enough light to make out more than that. We'd have to move the bike to get him free, but the edge of the ditch was too steep for us to be able to pull it out.

"We'll need to roll the bike off you," I said.

Alex nodded and winced.

I moved around to the other side while I decided whether to warn him that moving it could actually make things worse. His leg was pinned so tightly, the pressure might be stopping any serious bleeding. If we got the bike off him, he could bleed out quicker. Lucy watched me. I couldn't tell if she knew the risk we'd be taking.

"Okay, we're going to have to lift together from this side. We're only going to get one crack at this. Alex, we'll try to roll it over completely, but as soon as you're free, get out of the way. If you can."

He gave me a dubious look, but he nodded anyway.

Lucy and I crouched down beside the bike and felt around underneath for something to hold on to.

"Ready?" I said.

Lucy nodded.

"On three. One... two... three!"

We lifted the bike upward. My fingers slipped. Lucy yelped as the bike slid away from us. The dirt beneath our feet was loose, and my right foot twisted sideways.

"Lift!" I said.

I leaned forward, putting my weight behind the movement. The wheels caught, and the bike tipped. The metal frame dug into my hands as I pushed the bike forward. Lucy lost her balance and let out another yell. Alex screamed, but the bike's momentum carried it over, and it crashed into the opposite side of the ditch.

I knelt down beside Alex. His foot was twisted awkwardly, but there was no blood that I could see. His boot seemed to have protected him from more serious injury.

"Okay, your ankle's probably broken. It looks pretty clean, but you won't be running any marathons in the near future."

Alex snorted through gritted teeth.

The ditch was about four feet deep—just enough to make it hard for Alex to climb out.

"We need to get you up there," I said. "But it isn't going to be easy. It'll hurt."

"Can't you get... a stretcher? From the camp?"

"I didn't see one, and even if I had... Mike's been bitten."

Alex rolled his head back. "Oh crap..."

"You're going to be okay. *Both* of you," Lucy said.

"You're the boss," Alex said.

"You bet I am; now come on."

Lucy and I knelt on either side of Alex, our arms hooked beneath his. He screamed as we lifted him upright. For a few seconds, he looked like he was going to faint, then he swallowed, took a deep breath, and nodded. He leaned against me, keeping the weight off his broken ankle while Lucy climbed up to the trail to help him.

The sides of the ditch were steep, and the earth was dry. It crumbled away every time Alex tried to clamber out. Twice he ended up screaming in agony after sliding back down and knocking his injured foot.

In the end, he lay back against the slope, and I used my hands to provide a foothold. He managed to push himself part of the way up, and Lucy dragged him the rest. His broken ankle bounced against the edge of the ditch as she hauled him over the top. He screamed again, and I winced. If there were more zombies nearby, they'd be attracted by the prospect of convenient food. Alex leaned heavily into Lucy, but I still thought he was going to collapse. I managed to scramble out of the ditch and get my arm under his shoulder before he did.

We led him over to the remaining roadworthy bike. Mike was still leaning over the front. We approached him carefully, and when he raised his head, I reached for my knife. His eyes were clear, but his skin glistened in the sunlight, waxy and pale. He caught my eye, but I looked away. Lucy was still carrying her gun, and I had no doubt she'd use it.

Alex leaned back against the bike while I looked at his foot. The crash had twisted it to the right, and when I moved it slightly, he cried out in pain. His foot had swollen until it was wedged tight. I had no idea how we were going to get the boot off. Even if we cut the laces it was going to hurt like hell to remove it.

"How's it look, Doc? Will I play professional hockey again?"

At least his sense of humor was intact. "We can't do anything here; we'll have to get you back to the camp."

"I don't want to sound like a wimp, but I don't think I can walk that far."

"We can take the bike. The three of you can ride, and I'll walk along behind with as many of the supplies as I can carry. Assuming Lucy's okay to drive?"

She nodded.

"Good. Alex, you can sit behind Lucy. Mike? Will you be able to ride on the back?"

Mike raised his head and looked over his shoulder at me, but Lucy spoke first. "Yes, he'll be fine."

"We'd better get going. We don't have a lot of time."

I pulled the backpacks off the bikes and checked their weight while Lucy helped Alex and then Mike onto the bike. Mike sat on the rack, facing backward. They were both pale and in pain. Neither of them looked like they'd survive the journey back to the camp. I stashed the lightest of the backpacks next to the crashed bike and swung the other over my shoulder in the hope it would have the most useful contents. Maybe I could come back for the rest later.

Mike rested his injured arm in his lap and used the other to hold on to the rack.

Lucy started the engine.

"You'll need to take it slow," I said.

Mike leaned over his shoulder and called to Lucy. "Give Marcus the gun, Luce."

"No." Her voice was flat.

"Luce, I'm not letting you do this unless you give him the gun."

She held out until Mike started to climb off the bike.

"Here."

She held out the gun, but when I took hold of it she tightened her grip. She held my gaze for a few seconds until I understood her unspoken warning, then she released the weapon.

I removed the clip. It was empty. I showed it to Mike, and he gave a wry smile. He had another clip in a pocket on his belt. He threw it to me. I fumbled with it, trying to work out how it fit. When it eventually clicked into place, I slipped the gun into my belt. It felt awkward and heavy, as though it would fall out at any moment or just spontaneously go off. I removed it again and carried it instead.

Lucy accelerated slowly down the slope. Mike winced as the bike's movement jostled him. I walked behind, watching him closely as we rolled steadily toward the camp.

Chapter 34
MERCY

Lucy parked the bike outside the lodge and climbed off, immediately putting herself between me and Mike. She needn't have worried; I wasn't going to kill him. When she held out her hand for the gun, I gave it to her. I put the backpack on the walkway outside the lodge, grabbed the pair of the ski poles from the side of the building, and gave them to Alex. He swung his leg over the side of the bike and hesitantly stood up, using one of the poles to support himself. They were a little short for crutches, but they'd do.

Lucy moved to hook her arm under Mike's shoulder. He knocked her arm away. She stared at him.

"Guys, can you leave us alone for a minute?" Mike said.

"Sure," I said. "Come on, Alex."

I held the door open for him as he struggled up the steps and into the lodge. Lucy had already started crying again when I closed the door behind us.

I led Alex over to the couch and helped him sit down. Then I dragged the coffee table over and placed his foot on it. He hissed in pain but thanked me anyway.

"We'll need to get that boot off, but it's going to hurt."

Alex stared at his foot as though he was willing the leather and rubber to evaporate. "You need to deal with Mike first."

I let out a slow breath. I could hear Lucy and Mike talking, their voices too muffled by the lodge walls to be understood.

"You have to, Doc."

"I'm not a doctor."

"It's what he'd want."

I nodded.

We could hear Lucy shouting now, her voice filled with anger, frustration, and pain. She was begging Mike, pleading with him. I went to the window. He had his hands on hers, pressing the gun into them. She shook her head, but her shoulders sagged in resignation.

Tears streamed down her cheeks. She wiped at her face with her free hand then raised the gun. The barrel wavered as her shoulders shook. Mike said something, and she tensed, pulling herself upright, just a little.

I knew she couldn't do it even before she lowered the gun. I had no doubt she could kill. I'd seen her. But she couldn't execute the man she loved, not even to stop him from becoming a monster.

Lucy turned, the gun hanging limply at her side, and walked toward the lodge. She reached the walkway, and I opened the door.

Without saying anything, she held the gun out to me. I took it as she passed.

Alex watched us from the couch. Lucy sat down beside him, and he slung his arm around her shoulder.

"I'll be back in a couple of minutes," I said and swung the door shut.

The shadow roiled within my body, and I felt a glimmer of excitement. I'd been handed an opportunity. All I had to do was find a way to take advantage of it. If Mike sensed my excitement, he didn't show it. He just stood and waited for me.

"Not here," I said as I drew near. "It's too close. We'll go into the forest. I don't want them to see this."

Mike nodded.

He didn't speak as we made our way around the back of the lodge. I was grateful for the silence. The shadow surged through me, and I had to fight to keep it from overwhelming my senses. Trying to hold a conversation at the same time would have been all but impossible.

I don't think I realized exactly where I was taking him until we reached the path to the workshop. I pushed aside the bushes and directed Mike into the forest.

We walked until we were out of sight of the lodge, then I tapped him on the shoulder. "Here should be fine."

He turned to face me. In the shadow of the trees, his pale face almost glowed.

"Thank you," he said.

Unsure of what to say, I fiddled with the gun, checking the safety twice and then testing the feel of the weapon in my hand as though I were assessing the weight of fruit in a market.

Mike moved a few feet away, and I raised the gun. The shadow came forward, and I felt a rush of adrenaline. My trigger finger twitched. The barrel hardly moved. I took a deep breath and swallowed. Cold tendrils ran down my back, and I shuddered. I took another breath.

"I'm sorry. Could you...?" I spun my finger in the air.

Mike nodded.

He turned his back to me, pulling up straight. I stepped

forward and raised the gun until it was just a couple of inches away from the base of his skull. The world around me shrank, and the forest fell silent. It was just me and Mike.

"I'm sorry," I said and slammed the butt of the gun into the back of his head.

In the movies, that's enough to take a man down, but Mike just stumbled forward, yelling in surprise. I hit him again, putting all my weight into the blow. This time he fell, grunting as he fell to his knees. I hit him again, and he landed face-first in the dirt.

I raised the gun, ready to club him with it if he moved. He groaned a little then lay still. When I was sure he was out cold, I fired two shots off into the trees, sending birds scattering into the air. Then I slipped the gun back into my belt.

By the time Mike regained consciousness, I had him chained to the table in the workshop.

Chapter 35

MIKE

I stood beside Mike as confusion, surprise, and then anger passed over his face. He tried to sit up, but the chains across his neck, waist, and legs held him in place. He struggled, trying to break free, but the restraints were more than a match for his fading strength.

He looked at me, his brow furrowed. "What the hell?"

His voice was dry and weak, and his skin had taken on a plastic sheen. A spiderweb of thin black veins blossomed out around his eyes.

When I didn't reply, he started moving again. The chains rattled as he strained against them.

"If I were you," I said, "I'd rest. Concentrate on fighting the infection. It might buy you some more time."

He grunted. "I don't want more time."

"Suit yourself."

The gun was resting on the table behind me, well out of Mike's reach, but my knife was in my hand. I placed its tip on the end of my left index finger and raised it upright. I stared at it, letting it waver to and fro as though I was balancing it on my finger. The point was sharp, and I could feel it digging into my skin. A slight increase in pressure, and it would break the surface. I could picture it—a drop of red would bloom at the tip of my finger, and then the shadow would break free, bursting from my body in a column of darkness.

"Marcus, you don't need to do this."

His voice was still weak, but it was calm now. It was the polite, rational sound of a trained police officer trying to defuse a dangerous situation.

The shadow reached into my mind, and I smiled. "Don't waste your breath," we said.

I took the knife away from my finger and, still smiling, leaned forward until my face was directly over his. My knife hand was resting on the edge of the table. I could see him watching it, trying to work out whether he could make some sort of move before I rammed the blade into his skull.

"I have to go," I said. "I need to deal with Lucy and Alex."

Mike's eyes widened, and he shook his head, but I turned away before he spoke. I picked up the gun and weighed it in my hand as though I was debating what to do with it. Then I slipped it into my belt.

The chains rattled again as I walked away.

"Where are you going? Marcus, don't just leave me here. For God's sake. Please."

Mike's shouts grew louder and more urgent as I opened the door and walked out.

"You can't do this. Please, Marcus!"

I stood outside the workshop for a moment, letting the shadow drink in his fear, his panic. Then I swung the door closed. I slipped the knife back into its sheath and walked toward the trail to the camp, Mike's cries chasing me through the trees.

Chapter 36

FIRE

Lucy was waiting for me at the back of the lodge. She had an armful of branches.

"Thank you," she said. Her voice was flat, and when I looked in her eyes they were empty.

I nodded.

"I've started a signal fire," she said.

"No, we can't do that."

"I already have."

I stared at her for a moment then ran around the side of the lodge.

The fire pit was filled with wood and paper. The mound was already burning, orange-and-yellow flames flickering in the late afternoon light. A broad pillar of smoke rose up into the air. Lucy appeared beside me and threw the branches onto the fire. Smoke billowed from the pit, catching in my throat.

"But you were going to the ranger station."

"Alex is too badly hurt. There's no way he'd make it on foot, and we don't have enough fuel to use the bike."

I looked around us at the forest. "But the fire will bring people."

"That's the point, Marcus. We need help!"

"No!" I spun away and ran back to the lodge.

Alex was standing by the door, and I nearly knocked him over as I charged past. I grabbed a bucket from beneath the sink in the kitchen and filled it with water. As I hurried outside, the shadow berated me for my stupidity. I should kill them now, while Alex was injured and Lucy's guard was down.

But I needed to put out the fire first. I tapped my knuckles against the side of my head. "Shut up!"

Alex watched me with fear in his eyes as I crossed the living room and went outside. I brushed past Lucy toward the fire. She grabbed the bucket's handle. "No, Marcus."

"We can't have a fire," I said, almost spitting each word.

I yanked the bucket, freeing it from Lucy's grip. Water splashed across the ground. I threw the rest over the fire. The wood hissed and popped, but if anything the water just generated more smoke. I hurled the bucket across the camp in frustration.

I heard a rattle of metal. Two zombies stumbled out of the forest, near the trail that led back to the river. Fishing line from my perimeter was caught around their ankles, and they dragged a cluster of tin cans behind them.

I pulled the knife from my belt and moved toward them. Anger and frustration roared through my system. The shadow joined in, but its cries were of delight. I'd barely made it three steps when there were two loud bangs and the zombies fell to the ground. Lucy was standing just behind me, a pistol in her hands.

I pressed my hands against my forehead and looked toward the tree line. In my mind, I could see them out there in the shadows—a hundred, a thousand zombies swarming from the forest to tear us apart.

Something touched my shoulder, and I spun, my knife flashing in the waning sun.

"Easy, Marcus."

It was Lucy. Her left hand was held out, palm up, but I could see the gun in her right. It was ready if she needed it.

"It's okay," she said.

The fire had grown stronger, the flames flickering higher as they were fed by wood that had been drying in the summer heat for months. There'd be no putting it out now.

I clenched the knife. "Damn!"

"Shhh..." Lucy said.

I opened my mouth to respond, but she raised her hand. "Listen."

At first, all I could make out was the crackling of the fire. Then I heard it.

The low-pitched thumping of a helicopter's rotors.

Chapter 37

RESCUE

The chopper swept over the camp, the backwash sending smoke and dirt swirling into the air. It was gone in a matter of seconds. Lucy waved her arms over her head, shouting after it. I simply stood there, watching it circle around for another pass. With all the dust, smoke, and noise, it felt like the end of the world. At least for me.

The helicopter dipped its nose and flew toward the camp, slower this time. A machine gun was mounted in the aircraft's open doorway, and I could see the gunner. He pointed down then tilted the weapon toward us. Lucy was still waving her arms above her head and shouting for help even though they'd obviously already seen us.

The lodge door was open, and Alex stood there with a huge grin plastered all over his face.

The helicopter dropped lower until its skids were almost brushing the tops of the trees. The gunner leveled the machine gun at us. I could see the belt of ammunition hanging beneath the weapon, swaying with the motion of the helicopter. It was almost hypnotic.

The whine of the helicopter's engines shifted in pitch as

it slowed and then stopped, hovering above the open area behind the lodge.

Lucy ran past me. "Let's go!" Her voice was filled with excitement and relief.

I felt nothing but dread.

"Come on, Doc," Alex said.

He was still using the ski poles as crutches, but it didn't stop him from almost running along the walkway after Lucy.

The helicopter dropped out of sight.

Run, said the shadow, its voice so clear in my head it was as though it were standing beside me.

I almost did.

My feet took three steps toward the forest of their own accord. Only the thought of the workshop and the possibility that I'd lose the leather case stopped me. There was still a chance I could salvage the situation. If I could just deal with the helicopter.

I ran along the side of the lodge, grabbing another of the ski poles on the way. If I could somehow wedge it into the chopper's engine...

I dropped the pole as soon as I reached the clearing.

Lucy and Alex were standing a few feet away, hands raised above their heads, faces tilted downward to shelter from the debris being blown about by the helicopter. Two soldiers had taken up position near the aircraft and were kneeling, automatic rifles trained on Lucy and Alex. A third soldier was walking toward them with a pistol in his hand.

One of the kneeling soldiers turned her weapon toward me. I stopped moving and raised my hands.

The man with the pistol got to within ten feet of Lucy and Alex and then stopped. "Place your weapons on the ground," he shouted. His words were almost drowned out by the sound of the helicopter.

Lucy nodded and threw the gun away, well out of reach of all three of us. I removed my knife from my belt and did the same.

"My name is Captain Faraday."

"I'm Lucy, this is Alex, and that's Marcus."

"Is there anyone else here?"

"No... not anymore."

"Are you infected?"

"No."

The captain tapped his forehead. "What about that?"

Lucy raised her hand to her head. Blood was smeared across her forehead, and her hands came away sticky. "It's just a cut, an accident. Alex has a broken ankle, but we haven't been bitten."

"What about you?" Faraday said to me.

"I'm fine. One of us was bitten, but he's been dealt with."

The captain's eyes narrowed. I swallowed, trying to relax my face into what I hoped was a natural, and honest, expression.

"Captain!" shouted one of the soldiers.

A zombie had stepped out of the forest, drawn by the noise of the helicopter. It was a woman. By the state of her clothing, she'd been wandering around the wilderness for weeks. The captain nodded, and the soldier fired once. The back of the zombie's head exploded, and she collapsed to the ground. Behind her, three more zombies stepped into view.

"Zees on the right, sir."

"Dammit," said Captain Faraday. "Take them out."

Three more shots, and three more zombies dropped to the ground.

"Come on!" said Faraday, waving to us. "Get in."

Lucy and Alex ducked down and ran toward the helicopter.

I sensed rather than heard the zombie behind me and turned as he made a grab for my head. His movements were slow and clumsy. I sidestepped the attack and pushed him to the ground. There were two more zombies just behind him. My knife had fallen too far out of reach for me to get it. I backed away toward the lodge and Lucy's pistol.

More gunfire crackled around me, but the number of zombies was increasing. Lucy and Alex had reached the helicopter, and the soldiers were backing toward the door too. Captain Faraday waved at me to hurry up.

A female zombie shuffled into sight around the end of the helicopter. Captain Faraday fired at it. The shot hit her in the shoulder, making her stagger backward into the rear rotor blades. They ripped the back of her head off, splattering blood and bone across the side of the chopper before she fell forward into the grass.

The two soldiers climbed on board the helicopter and took up seats opposite Lucy and Alex. Faraday waved at me again as the whine of the helicopter's engine increased in pitch.

I'd reached Lucy's gun, and I bent down and picked it up. Another zombie appeared in front of me. I aimed the gun and fired. The weapon bucked in my hand, and the shot went wide. I fired again, this time hitting the ground at the zombie's feet. I moved toward the lodge, away from the helicopter. Alex was shouting at me, his words drowned out by the roar of the engine.

Something grabbed my arm. I twisted, bringing the gun up and firing as the zombie launched himself at me. The bullet tore through his shoulder, barely slowing him down. I screamed as his teeth clamped down on my arm. Panicking, I slammed the heel of my hand against his forehead and pushed.

My fingers slipped on rotten skin, but the pressure on my arm eased. I pulled away, rammed the pistol against his temple, and fired. The zombie's head exploded, blood spattering my face.

I clutched my arm and let out a cry of frustration. Faraday was on the helicopter now. He slowly shook his head at me then called back into the cockpit. The chopper wavered slightly then lifted off the ground.

Alex leaned from behind Faraday. He was shouting at the captain and pointing at me. Faraday shook his head. When Alex looked at me, there was despair written across his face. I slowly raised the gun and gave him a casual salute. He returned the gesture.

Another zombie stumbled into sight. I backed toward the lodge door, praying it was unlocked. Still clutching my arm, I fumbled with the handle for a few panicked seconds. Then there was a click, and the door swung open. I fell backward into the dining room, kicking the door shut behind me.

I leaned against the wall and sank to the floor. Outside, the sound of the helicopter grew louder. There was gunfire and the rapid chatter of the machine gun. Then the firing stopped, and the helicopter's engine faded away, leaving me in silence.

I looked down at my arm. The sleeve of my jacket was covered in blood and bile where the zombie had clamped itself on to me. I took a deep breath and slid the sleeve up, exposing my arm.

I smiled.

The bite hadn't made it through my jacket.

Chapter 38

ALONE AGAIN

I slept like the proverbial baby that night. Everything was so quiet, just the soft moaning of the zombies outside to lull me to sleep. Despite their presence, I felt perfectly safe. The lodge was well built, and they showed no signs of trying to get in. Maybe they thought I was dead, just as Lucy and the others did.

When I woke the next morning, I remembered the zombie's jaws clamping down on my arm, and a sudden burst of terror hit me. I hurriedly pulled up my sleeve. There was a large, oval bruise where the zombie had bitten me, but he'd failed to break the skin. It wasn't an experience I wanted to repeat, but I'd been lucky—both not getting bitten and having the opportunity to get rid of Lucy and Alex.

The farewell salute had been a nice touch, but maybe I should have fired a shot as soon as I got into the lodge—just to reinforce the impression that I'd taken my own life.

Looking through my bedroom window, I could see the bodies of fifteen or so zombies scattered around the grass. Another zombie, this one still walking, stood at the edge of the forest, staring blankly into the distance. Two more knelt by one of their fallen comrades.

I checked my gun. It still had three rounds in it, but there were probably more somewhere in the lodge. The shadow ran its fingers down my spine, and I shuddered. It whispered to me—*Mike*. In the excitement, I'd forgotten about him.

The sun was already out, and the room was warming up. I took a deep breath and stretched, savoring the cracking of my bones. Then I went downstairs, whistling as I took them two at a time, and made breakfast. After I'd eaten, I moved around the lodge, looking at the zombies outside.

I spotted six of them, but they were spread about, and they were all just standing motionless, waiting. I reloaded the gun, found another knife, and went outside.

There were two zombies standing near the fire pit. Maybe they'd been drawn there by the flames, perhaps driven by some remnant of their former selves to find warmth. Either way, they knew not to get close enough to catch light. A thin ribbon of pale smoke wound up into the sky, but that was all that was left of the fire now. I'd douse it once I'd dealt with the zombies.

I was able to get to the first one without being seen, and I rammed the knife into the base of his skull before he could react. The movement attracted the attention of the second zombie, a girl in a set of biker leathers. She'd obviously been in an accident. The right arm of her jacket was heavily scuffed and dotted with grit. The side of her skull had been torn away, exposing the brain within. It made her an easy kill.

As I pulled my knife from biker girl, I heard a muffled groan. Another zombie had appeared, one I hadn't seen on my initial reconnaissance. He was big, probably twice my weight. Thankfully, he was very slow. He lumbered toward me, and I ducked under his outstretched arms and drove the knife up into his jaw. He let out a wet, gargling cry and went limp. He dragged the knife from my grip as he fell, and I cursed as I retrieved it. I was getting careless. There were still at least four zombies near the lodge, and who knew how many more waiting in the forest. I needed to be more careful.

I moved around the buildings until I could see the entire clearing. The two zombies crouched over the corpse were actually eating it. They were picking at its flesh, gradually stripping the body to the bone. I'd never seen the phenomenon before. Every other zombie I'd seen had been seemingly oblivious to others of its kind.

The other zombie I'd seen earlier was still standing motionless at the edge of the forest. Another was near the path that led to the workshop. He was staring up at the trees, his mouth slack.

If I were a better shot with the pistol, I'd have used that to take some of them down. But as I'd proved the day before, I was no marksman, even at close range. It would have to be my knife.

Staying crouched, I ran across the clearing as quietly as I could, toward the zombie by the path. The grass brushing against my legs sounded incredibly loud, but he didn't hear me until I was almost on him. I caught him in the face, and the knife embedded itself in his right eye. My momentum carried the zombie over. I pulled the blade free as he fell and then slammed the heel of my boot into his face, shattering bone.

The feeding zombies were twenty feet away, but they'd seen me. They rose from the corpse, their movements languid. Bits of flesh clung to their faces from their meal.

Behind them, the slack-jawed zombie in the forest was still staring up at the trees.

My pulse was racing. I could feel the shadow delighting in the carnage, urging me on to bigger and bloodier things. I moved to the flattest piece of ground I could find, kicked a couple of rocks out of the way, and then waited for the zombies to come to me.

Both men wore identical outfits, were the same height, and despite the decay, their features were almost perfectly the same. They must have been twins. Their clothes had been beige originally, but now they were soaked with blood. One of them had a strip of pale flesh hanging from the side of his mouth—more remnants of their feasting. There was no sign of how they'd died. Their movements were slow and deliberate, and it gave me plenty of time to plan my attack.

The two of them reached me at the same time. The first twin went down with a single blow from the knife. I swept the point down onto the top of his head. It sank deep into his skull, but the zombie stayed upright. I pulled the knife free. He wavered slightly until I rammed my forearm against his chest. He fell, but in the time it had taken me to knock him over, his brother had gotten hold of me.

He clamped one hand around my arm and clutched at my throat with the other. I ducked forward. His fingers grazed my head, one ragged nail tearing across my scalp. I swung the knife upward. It sank into his arm, just below the elbow. Bone snapped.

The zombie let out a deep-throated cry of rage and clumsily tried to grab my face. This time, I was ready for him. I rammed the knife into his throat, cutting off the cry. I twisted the blade and pulled it free as he collapsed to the ground.

While I was fighting the twins, another zombie had

come out of the trees. She was old and decrepit. What few clothes she wore were torn and rotten, exposing the decaying flesh beneath. Ribs, stark against her gray skin, poked through split flesh.

She wobbled unevenly toward me, a tattered chunk of meat clutched in one hand. I steadied myself, and as she stepped into range, I swung the knife. The blade sank deep into the side of her head, and she fell to the ground. She lay there, twitching, making one last effort to cling to living death. Then she let out a soft moan and lay still.

The zombie near the path seemed completely oblivious to me. I walked right up to him, weapon at the ready, but he just stood there, looking up into the trees. I got as far as picking a spot on his neck for the knife when the shadow stopped me. I was wasting an opportunity. I could come back for him later.

I lowered my weapon and walked through the forest toward the workshop.

Chapter 39

TWO MEN REMAIN

Mike was still alive when I got to the workshop. Barely.

His skin was stretched tight over the bones of his skull, cheekbones clearly visible—diagonal slashes straining against the gray flesh. A few clumps of hair had fallen from his scalp. His lips were dry, and there was a split running down the middle of the lower one. A trickle of dark blood had run down his chin and pooled on his throat. It was almost black.

The shadow could see his guilt, and now so could I. He was corrupted by it. It rolled off him like great waves of black tar, and a black aura hovered around his body like heat haze. It wasn't the virus that was killing him; it was his guilt. The guilt that only the shadow could release.

He turned his head toward me. His eyes were dark, and the whites had almost been swallowed up by the blackness of the irises. Gray smudges ran beneath each one. A scarlet-and-purple welt cut across his forehead. He opened his mouth to speak, but no words came out.

"Good morning, Mike."

He tried to sit up, made it a few inches off the table, then fell back down. His head thumped onto the bench. The chains wrapped around him rattled.

I walked over to the shelves, past the snare hanging on the wall. Mike watched me as I moved. I placed the knife on the table. Its blade was slick with blood, the viscous black liquid dripping onto the table's pale wood.

I opened the drawer and removed the case containing my tools. The smell of leather drifted up to me. I closed my eyes and ran my fingers over the lid, savoring its touch. The shadow and I sighed. I opened the case and pulled out the fourth scalpel.

"Please..."

I turned to Mike. His mouth was open, and his tongue nestled inside, thick and black. It looked like he was eating a giant slug.

He swallowed and spoke again. "Marcus..."

His chest rose and fell. Each rattling breath was harsher and shallower than the last. He coughed. Thick black blood spattered the floor around the bench, barely missing my foot.

"Kill me..."

I crouched down beside the bench so that my face was a couple of inches from his. "You want to die?"

Mike dragged in another breath. "Y-Yes."

Even through the ragged breath, I could hear the desperation in his voice.

I held the scalpel in front of him and raised my eyebrows. He nodded. What little white remained in his eyes was tinged with red. I could smell him. He'd fouled himself, but there was a trace of decay beneath that bitterness—subtle but definitely there. He coughed again. Black phlegm dripped from his mouth. Perhaps he was already dead.

I reached over and rested the scalpel's blade on his throat. He tipped his head back and closed his eyes.

It would be so easy. I could increase the pressure until the blade sank into his flesh. I could drag it across his throat, freeing the guilt now flowing through his veins and corrupting his body. It wouldn't be enough, of course. I would have to decapitate him. That was what he really meant when he said he wanted to die. He didn't want to become one of them.

Anger flared—the shadow. I shouldn't waste this opportunity.

I removed the scalpel.

Mike opened his eyes. "No, please..."

Oil-stained tears ran down his face. He grimaced in pain. I expected him to beg me to kill him, but he didn't say anything.

Instead, he arched his back and groaned. His spine cracked, and the groans became a guttural scream of pain. Metal rattled as he writhed on the table, his face contorted in agony. The pain seemed to ease, and he relaxed again. His groans were replaced by ragged breaths.

I heard a noise—a sharp snap. It came from outside. Not close but still loud enough to break through the wheezing of Mike's final breaths. Another crack, closely followed by a rapid series of pops.

Gunfire.

It couldn't be the military. I hadn't heard the helicopter. *Unless it flew into the camp from another direction,* whispered the shadow.

"No." This was not happening.

Mike's eyes widened. He cried out. It was a strangled,

pathetic noise, but it might still be enough for someone outside to hear.

I paced along the side of the workbench, my hands pressed on top of my head. The shadow urged me to ignore the gunfire. I should just focus on the opportunity fate had presented me.

Mike struggled against the chains.

More shots cracked and popped. I was sure it was closer now. Whoever was in the camp was heading this way.

I slammed my hand against the table hard enough to rattle the knife. Pain shot up my arm and into my shoulder. I replaced the scalpel, closed the case, and jammed it into my jacket pocket. I reached for the knife. My hand stopped just above the handle. The shadow held it there. *Patience.*

My fingers were shaking, just slightly. Then another burst of gunfire broke the shadow's hold on me.

The shadow screamed in frustration as I grabbed the knife. I swept it upward as I turned and brought it down on Mike's neck. The blade tore through flesh and bone. His head tipped back, his eyes vacant. I sawed at his neck, slicing through flesh and severing his spine.

More gunshots drifted to me through the trees. I dropped the knife and ran out of the workshop.

Chapter 40

AIM FOR THE BRAIN

The military were back.

Four soldiers stood in the middle of the grassy clearing, more of the grunts like the ones that had been defending the helicopter. I didn't recognize them, and there was no sign of Captain Faraday or the chopper itself. A group of zombies had arrived in the camp as well, and the grunts were picking them off one by one. Machine-gun fire came from somewhere beyond the lodge.

I stayed out of sight, watching the soldiers gun down the zombies as they stumbled into the open. Even if I'd wanted to approach them, chances were they'd shoot me before I could show them I was still one of the living. If I was lucky, they'd clear out the camp and not find me or the workshop.

Another soldier appeared at the side of the lodge. She was wearing a heavy flak jacket and a metal helmet. Her clothes were streaked with black. She shouted at the four soldiers. Two of them peeled off and jogged across the grass to her, and then all three disappeared around the lodge.

A zombie, a lumbering hulk of a man, bare chested and with a wound in his stomach that had almost torn him in half, stumbled into the clearing. Both soldiers raised their guns and fired at the same time. The back of the man's head exploded, and he fell to the ground. The soldiers laughed, high-fiving each other before turning to sweep the clearing again.

There were no more zombies for the time being, but one of the soldiers, an intense-looking girl who barely seemed old enough to enlist, pointed toward the trees where I was hiding.

I ducked.

The gunfire I was expecting didn't come, but when I risked a peek through the undergrowth they were walking toward my hiding place. They hadn't seen me yet, but it was just a matter of time.

I brushed my hand against the knife on my belt and felt a spark of approval from the shadow. But there was a big differ-ence between a zombie and a trained soldier. I might take down one but not both of them. And they were armed. Their guns were lowered, but even so, there was no doubt in my mind that they'd put a bullet in my skull before I got anywhere near them.

Instead, I shouted. "Please don't shoot!"

Their weapons snapped to their shoulders. The nearest soldier dropped to one knee. The other stood, her weapon trained on the forest.

"Don't shoot," I said again.

The girl swept her rifle toward the sound of my voice. "Stand up. Very slowly."

I raised my hands and did as I was told. "I haven't been bitten."

Both of the soldiers were wearing earpieces that looked like Bluetooth headsets. The kneeling soldier touched his and said something I couldn't make out.

The girl flicked her rifle to the side. "Come out."

I picked my way through the undergrowth, being careful not to catch my foot on any of the roots or rocks that littered the ground. Sudden movements have a tendency to get people shot.

As I stepped into the clearing, the girl said, "That's close enough."

The woman in the body armor I'd seen earlier appeared from inside the lodge and walked across the clearing. She was accompanied by two more grunts, one on either side of her. She was unarmed apart from a pistol clipped to her belt, but her companions raised their automatic rifles as soon as they saw me. The sound of gunfire crackled through the trees around us.

She flicked her head at me. "Are you infected?"

"No, I'm not."

"Turn around. Slowly."

I did as I was told, painfully aware of the blood that was spattered across my face and clothes.

"Where did the blood come from?"

I had the irrational feeling that she'd somehow read my mind.

"I killed some of the zombies." I gestured toward the bodies scattered around the clearing. The soldiers tensed, and I raised my hands a little higher.

"You're the one the others told us about. They said you'd been bitten."

The soldier kneeling on the ground straightened, and I was sure his trigger finger twitched.

"Yes... no... I thought I was, but it didn't get through my jacket." I wanted to move my arm to show her, but it didn't seem like a good idea.

One of the grunts beside the woman turned to the right. "Sergeant, two zees at three o'clock."

The woman, the sergeant, didn't take her eyes off me. "Vantage, Robson. And don't forget, single rounds."

The two men flanking the sergeant took up position a few feet to the west. One of them fired two shots, and I heard the thud of a body falling to the ground. Three more shots and another thud.

The sergeant took a deep breath, annoyance flickering across her face. She nodded toward the soldiers aiming at me, and they lowered their weapons. "What's your name?"

"Marcus Black. Thanks for not shooting me."

"Don't thank me until we get you to safety."

"Oh right. Safety."

The sergeant smiled. "You can put your hands down now, Mr. Black."

I lowered my arms and let out a breath.

"Come on," said the sergeant. "Let's get you to the vehicles. There's a couple of Hummers parked outside the lodge."

Visions of a barbershop quartet flashed through my head, leaving confusion behind. "Hummers?"

"Yeah. Crappy gas mileage but damn near impregnable. At least as far as the zees go."

I smiled, my brain finally catching up with the meaning behind her words. Maybe I had been bitten after all.

"You didn't bring the helicopter?"

"No. That thing's gas mileage is even worse. Cleanup's done by a ground team. Just like the good old days."

The kneeling soldier raised his gun and fired off to my right. I ducked then moved out of the way as a zombie dragged itself out of the undergrowth. The soldier fired again, and the zombie's head exploded.

I hurried to the sergeant's side—partly to avoid any zombies but also to get out of the line of fire.

The sergeant pointed toward the workshop path. "Wentworth, there's a trail there. Take Davis and do a sweep, but this time, if it gets too hot, back out."

"Yes, ma'am," said the kneeling soldier.

"There's nothing down there."

"And what makes you think that, Mr. Black?" said the sergeant.

"I've just come that way. It's safe. That's why I was hiding there."

The sergeant shook her head. "There's a lot of forest for the zees to hide in. Go on, Wentworth."

I watched as the soldiers walked toward the trail. "There's really nothing—"

"Come on," said the sergeant. "Let's get you locked down."

She led me through the lodge with Vantage and Robson close behind. Soldiers were stationed in the living and dining rooms, with two more at the top of the stairs. They watched me as I passed. I tried to look relaxed, as though I was supposed to be there, but I could feel their suspicion hanging in the air around me. I was a civilian. I was a threat.

With each step I took, my spirit sank a little deeper. I'd regained my sanctuary only to have it snatched away again. I couldn't see a way out of this. I was getting a rescue I didn't want. The shadow had fallen silent.

There were over a dozen zombies lying on the ground around the camp. Most of them had come from the direction of the river, but a few were from the forest to the west.

Three more zombies broke through the tree line. Robson saw them and let off five quick shots, the bullets punching ragged little holes in the zombies' flesh until they went down and he stopped firing.

The Humvees the sergeant had mentioned were parked in the middle of the camp, near the fire pit. There were only two of them, but they were bigger than I'd expected. One was painted in the standard browns and greens of a military vehicle. The other was black, complete with tinted windows and spinning silver hubcaps. It wouldn't have looked out of place on the set of a rap video, apart from the tattered flesh hanging from its grill. One of the first soldiers I'd seen stood near the vehicles, and Vantage and Robson joined her.

The sergeant pointed toward the black Hummer. "Get inside."

"I really don't need rescuing."

"You don't have a say in the matter. Get in the vehicle." She was smiling, but the tone of her voice made it clear I wasn't going to be allowed to refuse.

The sergeant shouted at the soldiers, directing them to fan out and watch the perimeter. She gave the impression she wasn't paying any attention to me, but that was misleading. She was careful to keep me in the periphery of her vision as I moved toward the Hummer.

The vehicle's back door was slightly ajar, and I was about to pull it open when Davis ran around the corner of the lodge. I froze. She was carrying my snare. I touched the leather case through my jacket, drawing comfort from it.

"Sergeant Campbell!" she called.

Campbell directed Robson toward a group of zombies that were making their way down the road into the camp then turned to Davis.

I couldn't hear what they were saying, but after a few seconds Campbell looked across at me. She said something to Davis and took the snare. Davis walked back toward the clearing behind the lodge. Campbell looked at the snare then leaned it against the side of the Humvee. Then she removed her pistol from its holster and walked over to me.

"I'll give you one chance to explain what my team just found."

Chapter 41

INCOMING

I struggled to find the words that would satisfy Campbell. "I... I don't know..."

"Wrong answer." She raised her pistol. "Turn around, and put your hands on the vehicle."

"But..."

Campbell flicked the gun. "I won't ask again."

I turned and placed my hands against the Humvee. She pulled my knife from its sheath then called Vantage over.

"Check him."

Vantage patted me down and found the case. He pulled it out of my jacket and passed it to Campbell. She opened it, and I caught the familiar glint of silver. I thought I was going to vomit. She closed the box and threw it into the front of the Humvee.

"Put your hands behind your back."

I did as I was told. Campbell slipped a circle of plastic around my wrists and pulled it tight. She spun me around and pushed me against the Hummer. "Stay with him. If he moves, shoot him in the head."

Vantage nodded and raised his gun until it was pointing

at my face. The look in his eyes showed me he didn't need to be told twice.

Gunfire erupted off to our left. Campbell swore. She pressed her finger against the headset in her ear. "Everyone fall back to the vehicles. I repeat, fall back. We're getting out of here."

"Errm... Sergeant," I said.

When Campbell looked at me I nodded toward the road leading into the camp. Five more zombies were moving toward us, and I could see more, dozens more, outlined among the trees. Campbell ran to the front of the Humvee and retrieved an automatic rifle. She raised it to her shoulder and fired.

Three soldiers ran out of the lodge. They hesitated slightly when they saw the zombies then raised their guns and started firing.

I'll give him credit, Vantage wasn't distracted by the battle raging around him. He kept his gun trained on me. I'm not sure he even blinked.

"I don't want to tell you how to do your job," I said. "But it looks like your friends could do with some help."

Vantage didn't reply. Behind him, one of the soldiers pulled a grenade from his belt and threw it at the clump of zombies coming down the road. It rolled into the middle of them and exploded. Chunks of flesh flew through the air, hitting the trees and scattering across the ground. More zombies staggered out of the forest, replacing the ones taken out by the grenade.

Gunfire echoed across the camp.

Someone screamed.

I raised my eyebrows. "If that's a swarm, there's a good chance we aren't getting out of here alive."

This time, doubt flickered across Vantage's face.

I twisted, showing him my bound wrists. "I'm not going anywhere."

"You try something, and I'll take you down."

"Understood."

Vantage backed away then turned to face the oncoming zombies. He fired, his teeth clenched as the weapon in his hands bucked and the creatures fell. There was another explosion. It came from the far side of the camp this time and was followed by more gunfire.

Campbell shouted orders over the noise, directing her team to form a perimeter around the vehicles.

I moved my hands, searching for a piece of metal sharp enough to cut through the plastic around my wrists. The door was the best I could manage. I leaned against it and ran the restraint up and down its edge.

More explosions, this time accompanied by the sound of splintering wood. One of the lodge's windows exploded, scattering debris across the ground.

A soldier stumbled out of the lodge, his face twisted in fear. He backed down the walkway, firing into the building as he went. His gun swung from side to side, the shots scattering wildly. I couldn't tell whether he was hitting anything, but I could see the lumbering shape of a zombie advancing toward him out of the lodge.

And then the soldier's foot caught the edge of the walkway, and he went down. Bullets sprayed across the side of the building as he fell. The zombie lunged forward and landed on top of the soldier before he could get his weapon pointing in the right direction. The zombie clamped down on the soldier's throat, cutting off his screams.

Too late, Campbell rounded the corner of the Humvee and opened fire. Bullets tore through the zombie's shoulder then his skull. As the zombie fell away, she fired one more shot. The bullet hit the soldier in the side of the head.

Campbell turned, firing past me toward the road.

"Sergeant!" I said. "I can help." I half turned my back on her and wiggled my hands to remind her she'd handicapped me. "Please."

She hesitated, and a zombie staggered around the corner of the Humvee. One arm was missing, its shoulder a ragged mess of blood and gristle.

"Look out!" I said.

She turned and swung the butt of her rifle. It caught the zombie in the side of the head and knocked him to the ground. She slammed the heel of her boot into his skull. There was a hollow crack as it shattered.

Campbell raised her gun and fired at something out of my view then ran to me. She removed my knife from her belt and cut the plastic ties from around my wrists. After a slight pause, she gave me the knife.

"Do you know how to use a gun?"

I nodded, hoping I looked confident.

"Good," she said and handed me her pistol.

Vantage appeared. He saw me holding the gun, and I half raised my hands, trying to show him I wasn't a threat before he shot me.

He glared at me and then said, "Robson's down and out."

Campbell clenched her teeth and pressed a hand against her headset. "Davis? Come in, Davis?"

Vantage pointed. "There!"

Davis was just backing into view around the side of the lodge. She was holding her rifle at her hip and firing short bursts at targets we couldn't see.

"Davis!" said Campbell.

Still firing, Davis turned. There was a metallic clang and

then a deafening thump. The side of the lodge was torn apart as the generator exploded. Wood and dirt and fire rained down on the camp. Davis screamed and clutched her face, blood pouring from a gash in her cheek. Vantage ran to her side and slipped an arm under her shoulder, guiding her back to the Humvee.

"Hold them off!" said Campbell, and she climbed into the vehicle's cab.

The road was a mass of zombies. I raised the pistol and fired off a couple of shots. One of them went down; another staggered backward. With so many of them crowded into one place, it was hard to miss.

Fire spread through the lodge, the flames eagerly swallowing up the dry wood. Smoke drifted across the camp, hindering visibility.

The Humvee's engine roared to life, adding more noise and smoke to the scene. I fired again, hitting another zombie in the chest. There was a flash and the sound of gunfire from within the Humvee. Campbell screamed in anger and pain.

A pause.

Another shot rang out, and blood splashed against the driver's window.

"No!" said Vantage. He slipped his arm from beneath Davis's shoulder and ran around the front of the Humvee, firing as he went.

Still holding her hand to her cheek, Davis fired at the zombies swarming down the road. Following her lead, I raised the pistol and fired. Again and again, I pulled the trigger, the pistol jerking in my hand until I heard the dull click of an empty clip. I don't know if I hit anything.

Davis had switched to single shots. She was down on

one knee, picking off the zombies with finely placed rounds. Vantage was nowhere to be seen.

Find the case, whispered the shadow.

My eyes were streaming, and I could barely see. A zombie broke through the wall of smoke from the direction of the lodge. His back was on fire, creating a yellow aura around him. I shouted to Davis, and she turned and fired. The bullet hit him in the chest, knocking him over. Her rifle clicked empty. The burning zombie got back to its feet and staggered toward us. Davis threw her weapon away in frustration.

"Come on!" I said and moved around to the side of the Humvee.

Vantage was lying on the ground about twenty feet away, four zombies clustered around him. He was facing me, dull eyes staring lifelessly into mine as the creatures tore into his stomach. The corpse of a zombie lay on the ground nearby, a single bullet wound in his head.

Davis joined me. Her skin was pale, and her neck was awash with blood from the wound in her cheek.

"What now?" she said.

The shadow flashed a parade of images in my mind—me pushing Davis toward the pack of zombies. Her screaming in agony as she was torn apart by the swarm, the distraction giving me time to escape.

"Hold on."

The Humvee's window had been blown out. Blood and broken glass was splashed around the inside. I pulled open the door, and Campbell's body tumbled to the ground. Davis cried out. The back of Campbell's skull was missing where she'd taken her own life—her response to the ragged bite mark on her arm.

Another zombie lay motionless across the passenger

seat where it had clambered in through the open door. There was no sign of my case.

Clenching my teeth, I leaned inside and pushed the zombie out of the way. Its head lolled sideways. Instinctively, I pulled back, away from its snapping jaws, but the side of the creature's face was missing, and it was dead. I caught a glimpse of brown in the footwell. My case had fallen off the seat and slid almost out of sight.

I checked over my shoulder. The smoke was making it hard to see what was going on, but I could hear the moans of the zombies above the crackle and pop of the burning lodge. My head pounding, I climbed into the Humvee and reached for the case.

Gunfire exploded somewhere off to my left, and I slipped. I fell forward. In other circumstances the sight of my legs flailing around in midair as I tried to right myself might have been funny. All I could think of was how tempting I would look to the zombies out there in the smoke.

My fingers grazed the edge of the case. I just about managed to drag it out from beneath the seat. Black blood was smeared across the lid, but otherwise, it looked intact. I hurriedly pushed myself back out of the Humvee. Davis watched me put the case into my jacket pocket, the look on her face a mix of anger and amazement.

"That way," I said, pointing between the two nearest cabins.

The path seemed clear, at least for now. Davis nodded and ran.

I slipped my knife into my belt and grabbed my snare.

Chapter 42

BLOOD AND SMOKE

We sprinted through the smoke.

Halfway to the cabin, I tripped over a soldier's corpse, Robson maybe. I stumbled and almost dropped the snare.

A shape rose up in front of me—a massive man in a military uniform with a ragged hole in the center of his chest. Bizarrely, the only thought that went through my mind was that I couldn't see how he'd have fit in a Humvee.

Then the shadow took over, and I swung the snare. The blade I'd bolted to the end of the pole slashed across the man's throat. Slicing it open released a wave of black tar. He grabbed at me, but he was slow, and I ducked beneath the attack. I jabbed the snare forward. The blade sank into the man's cheek. I felt it hit bone, yanked it back, and then jabbed it at his face again. It pierced his eye.

The zombie roared. I attacked again, but this time he knocked the snare away. The pole was long and unwieldy, and I struggled to get it back under control as the giant man closed on me. Then he slammed his fist into the side of my head.

I fell sideways, my head ringing from the blow. The zombie came at me. I tried to swing the snare toward him again, but he was too close. The pole hit him in the leg, but he didn't react or slow his approach. I dropped the snare and pushed myself backward, desperately trying to get out of his path.

He took a few steps then collapsed onto his knees. The damage I'd done was finally having an effect. Then his hand clamped around my calf. I yelled out as he dragged himself toward me, his clawlike fingers sinking into my flesh. I fumbled with my knife, and it almost slipped from my fingers.

There was a blur of brown, and a booted foot slammed into the zombie's head. It snapped left, and he let out a moan. Davis kicked again. The zombie's grip around my calf loosened, and I pulled myself free.

The massive zombie reached for Davis. I lunged at him and drove my knife into the top of his skull. Still refusing to die, he swung an elbow at me. It connected with the corner of my eye. Stars burst across my vision. I fell back and began kicking, desperate to block any attacks coming my way, but he'd finally stopped moving. Thick black blood poured from around the edges of the knife still embedded in his skull.

Davis gripped my arm and pulled. "Come on!"

Another explosion roared from somewhere behind us, the vehicles or more of the lodge going up in flames.

I forced myself to my feet, and we ran, weaving between the cabins and into the forest. There was no trail, and we had to push our way through the undergrowth. Brambles tugged at our clothes and skin. Progress was slow and noisy.

Davis's shoulder was soaked in blood, and she held her arm limply at her side. She was breathing heavily, and her forehead was drenched with sweat. The cut in her cheek was still bleeding, albeit slower now.

I pointed to our right where a pair of zombies were pushing their way through the forest. We crouched, both ready to run if we needed to, but they were moving away from us, toward the noise and excitement of the camp.

When the zombies were out of sight, we started moving again, sporadic gunfire and the screams of the dying echoing through the forest around us.

Chapter 43

A WAY TO LIVE

We pushed on until we found a narrow trail. It wound through the forest, heading south. There was no sign of any zombies. Davis's breathing came in ragged gasps. Several times she stumbled, tripping over her own feet.

The trail broke through a ring of trees into a small clearing. A stream, almost completely dry, ran through its center. Davis stumbled forward and dropped to her knees. She pressed her hand against her injured shoulder, closed her eyes, and took a deep breath.

"Aargh!" she said, her vehemence making me flinch.

"We'll rest for a few minutes."

Davis shook her head.

"You need to rest. We both do."

Davis shifted position until she was sitting down. Still clutching her shoulder, she shook her head again. "You're going to leave me here."

"No, I'm—"

Davis removed her hand. A ragged lump of flesh had been torn away from her shoulder, revealing the muscle and bone beneath it. Blood still pulsed from the wound, but the edges were already turning black.

"I... I'm sorry."

Davis let out a little snort. "So am I." Grimacing, she said. "You should go now."

"Don't you want me to..."

She swallowed. "No. I think I'd like to stay here awhile."

I felt a pang of unexpected emotion, sympathy maybe.

There was nothing I could say that wouldn't sound hollow. Instead, I nodded, my lips pressed tight. We sat in silence for a few minutes while I struggled to think of something to say, but it was Davis who finally spoke, her voice barely audible. "You should go. Please."

I looked around at the clearing. It was pretty. Secluded. She wouldn't be disturbed.

I offered her my hand, and she shook it. "Thank you," I said. "For saving my life."

"It's my job."

I smiled slightly and stood.

Davis lay back on the ground and stared up at the sky. I waited, trying one last time to think of the right words to say. Then I turned and walked toward the forest.

As I reached the edge of the clearing, Davis called to me. "Marcus?"

"Yes."

"What happened at the workshop?"

I turned back. She was still lying on the ground, her head tilted so that she could see me.

"I found a way to live as myself," I said.

Davis smiled, but her face was full of sorrow. She nodded slightly before looking back up at the sky.

I watched her for a moment. Then the shadow and I turned and walked into the forest.

Thank you for reading *Serial Killer Z*, I hope you enjoyed the book.

I've always had a soft spot for zombies. *Return of the Living Dead* is one of my favorite movies, and *The Walking Dead* is one of the few TV shows on my "must see" list. But other than a couple of very short stories, I'd always shied away from writing about them. Zombies are extraordinarily popular but it's hard to bring something new to the genre without losing the elements that make zombies so much fun.

Even when the idea of throwing a serial killer into the zombie apocalypse came to me (in the gym of all places), I resisted. But the idea just wouldn't let go. Pretty quickly that basic premise had grown into a series of books and, eventually, I gave in and started writing. I'm glad I did. It turns out writing about a serial killer and zombies is a lot of fun. I'm four books into the series so far, and I'm loving writing them.

Of course, writing a book is only the first step in the journey to publication and this particular book had a long and tumultuous birth involving multiple editors, theft, fraud, and various other unsavoury twists and turns. If we ever meet, buy me a drink and I'll tell you all about it.

The fact that this book exists after all the drama is down to the sterling work of my editor, Jason Whited, and my proofreaders at Red Adept Editing and Pikko's House. Thank you.

And a special thank you to James, a zombie enthusiast and good friend of mine who was kind enough to read an early draft of the book and give me feedback. It's a better book as a result.

If you'd like to find out how the zombie apocalypse started and what part Marcus played in it, you can get a free copy of the prequel novella, *Infection*, by signing up for my newsletter at http://smarturl.it/SKZNews. Subscribers also get discounted and free books, behind-the-scenes extras, and all sorts of other goodies.

Marcus's story continues with the next book in the series —*Serial Killer Z: Sanctuary*. It's another rollercoaster of a ride through the zombie-infested world with some fiendish twists and turns. And zombies. Lots of zombies.

Sanctuary is available right now from all your favourite retailers.

ABOUT THE AUTHOR

Philip Harris is a speculative fiction author and video game developer. Originally born near Oxford, England, he now lives on the West Coast of Canada where he spends his days developing video games and his nights writing speculative fiction—anything from horror to science fiction to fantasy.

His first publication, Letter From a Victim, appeared in the award-winning magazine, *Peeping Tom*, in 1995. His published books include *The Leah King Trilogy* and an homage to the old pulp science fiction serials—*Glitch Mitchell and the Unseen Planet*.

His short fiction has appeared in numerous anthologies and magazines including *The Jurassic Chronicles*, *Tales from the Canyons of the Damned*, *Bones*, *Uncommon Minds*, and *The Anthology of European SF*.

He has also worked as security for Darth Vader.

For up-to-date information on new releases, free ebooks, and other exclusive extras, please sign up to the mailing list at http://smarturl.it/SKZNews.

www.solitarymindset.com
philip.harris@solitarymindset.com